DISCOVER

READ

EXPLORE

LEARN

NEW HANOVER COUNTY
PUBLIC LIBRARY

SLIDE

JILL HATHAWAY

BALZER + BRAY
An Imprint of HarperCollins*Publishers*

Balzer + Bray is an imprint of HarperCollins Publishers.

Slide

www.epicreads.com

Library of Congress Cataloging-in-Publication Data
Hathaway, Jill.
Slide / Jill Hathaway. — 1st ed.
    p.   cm.
Summary: Vee Bell, able to slide into other people's minds, sees someone standing over the body of her sister's best friend, Sophie, holding a bloody knife, but she is afraid that anyone she tells will think her crazy, so she must find a way to identify the killer herself before he or she strikes again.
ISBN 978-0-06-207790-5
[1. Murder—Fiction.   2. Psychic ability—Fiction.   3. Sisters—Fiction.   4. Secrets—Fiction.   5. High schools—Fiction.   6. Schools—Fiction.   7. Best friends—Fiction.   8. Friendship—Fiction.   9. Narcolepsy—Fiction.]   I. Title.
PZ7.H2827Sli 2012   2011024551
[Fic]—dc23   CIP
                                                                                AC

Typography by Erich Nagler
12 13 14 15 16   LP/RRDH   10 9 8 7 6 5 4 3 2 1
❖
First Edition

For my mother,
who instilled in me a love of words,
and my daughter,
for whom I hope to do the same

CHAPTER ONE

'm slumped at my desk, fighting to keep my eyes open. A drop of sweat meanders down my back. It's got to be eighty-five degrees in here, though it's only October. When we complained, Mrs. Winger mumbled something about waiting for a custodian to come fix the thermostat.

Beside me, hunched over his desk, Icky Ferris stumbles through the words in *Julius Caesar*. We're supposed to be reading in partners—but his monotonous tone, paired with the unintelligible Shakespearean language that gets English teachers all hot and bothered, makes me feel unbearably sleepy.

Heat is one of my major triggers—and, apparently, so is Shakespeare. Warmth crawls up my spine like a centipede. It reminds me of the time I was sitting in my dad's car in August with the seat warmer accidentally on.

All the words in my book mush into blurry gray lines, and I know it won't be long before I lose consciousness. The room starts to turn inside out, the seams pulling apart. I pick something in the room to focus on and end up staring at an inspirational poster with a picture of a kitten hanging off of a tree branch. The caption reads: HANG IN THERE, BABY! As I watch, the kitten's face starts to melt. I slip down in my chair.

There are certain signs I'm about to pass out: drooping eyelids, muscles gone slack like spaghetti, a blank look on my face. My classmates have seen it enough times to be able to tell what's happening.

"Sylvia," Icky hisses, and then he claps in front of my face. "Snap out of it." I blink and focus on him. Icky has a mullet and an unhealthy obsession with firearms, but I like him. He certainly shows more compassion than most of the kids at my school. "You okay?"

By now, everyone's staring. It's not really a big deal anymore, me passing out in the middle of class, but it *is* something to break up this boring October day. There hasn't been any new gossip since the drug dogs found a bag of weed in Jimmy Pine's locker—and that was two weeks ago. I'd like to avoid losing myself completely in front of these vultures if at all possible.

I hoist myself out of the chair and approach Mrs. Winger, my English teacher. She's totally engrossed in something on her computer—probably solitaire. She's the only one who *didn't* notice me almost pass out. Her big desk is tucked in the very back of the room so she can ignore us. Pair by pair, my classmates' eyes drop away from me and go back to their reading.

"Can I go to the bathroom?" I make my words small and humble.

She doesn't bother to remove her eyes from the computer screen. If she did, she might see that it's me, Sylvia Bell with the narcolepsy issue, and remember she's been asked to let me leave the classroom whenever I need to.

Come on. Just let me go. LEMME GO.

The room spins and my knees start to buckle.

"Can't it wait until class is over?" Mrs. Winger's voice is snippy, cutting me into tiny pieces she can easily brush into the trash. She moves a stack of cards with her mouse.

"Can't your game wait until class is over?" I push a lock of pink hair behind my ear. I know it's a bitchy thing to say, but screw it. It's the only way to get her attention.

She finally looks my way, irritation deepening the lines around her eyes. "Fine. Go. Five minutes."

I don't respond because I'm already out the door. I should go to the nurse, but she's required to notify my father of any episodes, and I don't feel like dealing with the questions. Not today. I'm so tired. Sleep might stalk me throughout the day, but it evades me at night. Last night, I might've gotten a total of four hours of sleep.

On my way to the bathroom, I pray it's empty. No such luck—when I push open the door, I see a girl on her knees in the last stall, alternately sobbing and retching. I recognize the silver flip-flops. It's Sophie Jacobs, the only one of my little sister's friends I can stand. At least she won't tell anyone about my episode. She has her own secrets to keep, anyway, like the breakfast she was probably just getting rid of.

I lean against the wall and search the pockets of my hoodie for the little orange bottle—the one that's labeled

PROVIGIL. My doctor prescribed it to keep me awake, but in actuality it doesn't do crap. I've dumped out the Provigil and filled the bottle with cheap caffeine pills, the only drug that seems to work for me—and then only if I take about six of them at once. The Provigil makes me feel like I'm fighting my way through a fog, but the caffeine brings everything into focus. My hands shake as I fish out a few of the ovals and pop them into my mouth, even though I have a feeling it's too late.

The toilet flushes, and the stall door behind me swings open. Sophie just stands there, glassy-eyed, wiping her mouth with the back of a trembling hand. Her glossy black hair has a chunk of something yellow in it. I have to look away.

"Gah, I'm glad it's you," she says. She comes forward and twists the one knob above the sink. Our school doesn't so much have hot or cold water, just one temperature: arctic. She scoops some water into her hands and splashes her face. "I've been feeling sick lately."

I open my mouth to respond, but all that comes out is this weird rasp. My head aches. The room darkens, and I press my palms into my forehead, sinking to the floor.

I can never get used to the feeling of looking through someone else's eyes. It's as if each person sees the world in a slightly different hue. The tricky part is figuring out who the person is. It's like putting together a jigsaw puzzle— what do I see, hear, smell? Everything is a clue.

What I smell now: mildew and hair spray.

I'm in the girls' locker room. Hideous pink lockers line the walls. The girl I've slid into pulls black ballet flats onto her orangey, fake-tanned feet. Her toes are painted robin's-egg-blue with little daisies in the center.

Gym class must be over. Half-naked girls rush around, wiggling out of shorts way too skimpy for October, brushing their hair, discreetly swiping on powdery-smelling deodorant.

A few feet away, I recognize a blond girl sliding a pair of skinny jeans over her hips. She has a little white patch in the shape of the Playboy bunny on her hip, where she puts a sticker when she tans. The girl is Mattie. She is my sister and my exact opposite in every way. If she's the pink glitter on your valentine, I'm the black Sharpie you use to draw mustaches on the teachers in your yearbook.

I feel my mouth open, and out comes the voice of Amber Prescott, my least favorite person in the galaxy. "Ugh. I just got the worst headache. It came out of nowhere. Do you have any aspirin?"

My mind races. How could I have slid into Amber? I wasn't touching anything of hers. Was I?

Mattie fastens her silky ponytail with an elastic band. "Nope. Sorry. Anyway, it's really none of my business if Sophie wants to hook up with Scotch. She can go around acting like a whore if she wants."

"Personally, I think it's disgusting the way she's throwing herself at him. I mean, that's not what a good friend does. She *knew* you had a crush on him."

Scotch? As in Scotch *Becker*? The biggest prick in the

junior class? The mere mention of his name makes me feel like puking. When did Mattie start liking Scotch, first-string quarterback and douche extraordinaire?

Mattie's face puckers as if she's eaten a whole box of Lemonheads, which it always does when she's trying to act like something doesn't bother her.

"Well, what am I supposed to do? I can't force him to want me. And, duh, why wouldn't he like Sophie? She's . . . like . . . amazing-looking." Mattie drops onto the bench and covers her face with her hands.

Amber slithers closer to Mattie and pats her back. "Don't give me that shit, Mattie. Scotch is crazy for choosing that heff over you. I mean, Sophie can't go five minutes without sticking her finger down her throat. Just because she's lost about half her body weight doesn't mean she's not still fat *inside*. She's still Porky Pie from the sixth grade."

Porky Pie. Sophie's old nickname brings back memories, none of them good. Kids throwing oatmeal cream pies at her on the bus. The time in the computer lab when Scotch Becker pulled up the dictionary website and made the robotic voice say "hippopotamus" at her, over and over. I can't believe Sophie would even speak to Scotch after the things he did to her in middle school. In fact, I can't believe she speaks to Mattie or Amber. They only started hanging out with her after she lost weight, and even now Amber's favorite pastime is thinking of new ways to torture Sophie. Amber is forever pulling crap like telling Sophie her (nonexistent) ass looks fat or asking if Sophie should really be eating that slice of pizza. It's obvious she's completely jealous that Mattie and Sophie have become such close friends. She's seizing this opportunity to drive the two apart.

Mattie peeks at Amber through her fingers. "Do you really think so?"

"Don't worry," Amber says, pulling out a hot-pink cell phone. "I've got a plan to put her back in her place."

"Sylvia? Vee! Are you all right? Should I get the nurse?" Sophie hovers over me, twisting her hands in worry.

The bathroom tile is cool against my cheek. I wonder when they last mopped it. Pushing myself into a sitting position, I banish the visions of squirming bacteria from my thoughts.

"Ugh, no. I'm fine."

"Oh, God. Your forehead!"

I reach up and feel a huge lump.

Sophie tears several paper towels from the dispenser and holds them under the faucet. She gently compresses the cool, wet paper to my head. She's so freaking maternal. Last fall, when she and Mattie shared a birthday party, she made a chocolate cake from scratch. She covered it with chocolate icing and spelled out "Mattie" with M&M's. Mattie gave Sophie a Twinkie on a paper plate.

Just thinking about that party depresses me. Sophie is so sweet, really, despite her friends—including my sister, who used to be innocent and kind but in the last year has turned into such a bitch. I blame it on Amber.

Poor Sophie. She has no idea that, right this second, her

two so-called BFFs are talking shit about her. And evidently planning something to "put her in her place." I want to warn her to be careful around those two, but how would that look—me bad-mouthing my own sister? Would she even believe me?

Sophie pulls me to my feet. I lean against the sink and pull the paper towel away to assess the damage in the mirror. My forehead doesn't look too bad. I feel the bump gingerly. A minor contusion. Maybe my father won't notice.

Sophie meets my eyes in the mirror. "Are you sure you're okay?"

I turn to face her. Her shoulders are hunched, her head bowed. Her legs are two sticks beneath her cheerleading skirt. She can't weigh more than a hundred pounds.

"Yeah, I'm okay. Really. How are *you*?"

She gets this funny look on her face, and I'm not sure if she's about to start laughing or bawling.

"It's my birthday," she says finally, shrugging. "Mattie hasn't said anything. You can give this to your sister. I made it." Sophie holds out a braided friendship bracelet, the kind you make at summer camp. It's red and gold to match their cheerleading uniforms.

I can guarantee with near certainty that Mattie hasn't done anything special for Sophie's birthday. Again, I'm struck with the urge to tell Sophie to wise up and get some better friends. Thinking of how to phrase my words, I push the bracelet onto my wrist so I won't lose it.

"Sophie . . ." I say, taking a step toward her, but she ducks into the hallway before I can reach her, tears streaming from her eyes. I crumple the paper towel in frustration and aim for the garbage can. It misses by a mile. When I lean over to retrieve it, a dollar bill falls out of the pocket of my hoodie.

Crap. That must be why I slid into Amber.

Suddenly it all comes rushing back—Amber running up to me before first period, waving the crumpled dollar bill in my face.

"The stupid pop machine isn't taking my money," she'd wailed. "Caffeine is urgent. Do you have change?" She was completely freaking out, enough to leave an emotional imprint on the money she was holding, enough for me to pick up on less than an hour later.

I'd found a few coins for her and accepted the dollar in return, which I stuck in my pocket. I must have brushed against it when I reached for the Provigil bottle—just when I was feeling faint, just when I was vulnerable. If I put the money back in my pocket, I could accidentally slide into Amber again later.

Unwilling to take the chance, I use a paper towel to pick up the dollar, and then I toss it into the trash. I never want to be inside Amber Prescott's head again.

CHAPTER TWO

I speed-walk past the student entrance and almost run into Rollins, my best friend, who has a tendency to show up at school about halfway through first period.

"Vee!" He laughs and grabs my arm. "Where you off to in such a hurry?"

"Back to class," I say, turning my face away from him so he won't see the bump on my forehead. It's no use, though. Rollins sees everything.

"Hey," he says. "Hey. Stop."

I let him look me over, waiting for the inevitable questions. Things between us have seemed strained lately. It's as if Rollins senses that I'm hiding something. He keeps pushing, and I keep pulling away. If only he'd just let me be. . . .

Rollins shakes his long brown hair out of his eyes. "Are you okay? Did you just—"

"Mr. Rollins," a smug voice calls out. "Little late today, I see." Mr. Nast—"Nasty," to the students—strolls toward us, his thumbs tucked casually through his belt loops like he's in some kind of Western. It's the last face-off—Nasty, the principal, and us, the delinquents.

Nasty glares at Rollins, whose face has settled into a smirk. Rollins's snarky attitude hasn't won him any favors with the administration—that's for damn sure. He gets busted once a week on average. It's pretty much Nast's hobby, trying to nail Rollins for smoking in the parking lot or cutting class.

When Nast sees me, his face kind of wavers. I'm a tricky one. With my strange disability and permanent hall pass, there's not much he can do to me. Rollins, however, is a totally different story. I know for a fact he's only one tardy away from suspension.

Rollins's grip on my arm tightens for a moment, and then he lets go. He prepares himself for battle, crossing his arms over his chest and tightening his jaw.

I throw myself between them. "Mr. Nast, Rollins was just walking me to the nurse. I'm feeling faint." I make my voice wobbly and grasp Rollins for support.

Mr. Nast looks from me to Rollins and back again. I see in his face that he doesn't believe me, but there's nothing he can do. Finally he narrows his eyes and mutters to hurry up.

Rollins and I bustle away from him, arms linked, heading toward the nurse's office. When we round the corner, we burst into laughter, and any tension there might have been between us before has dissipated.

"I never knew you were such a fine actress," Rollins says, snorting.

"Oh, that wasn't an act. I really am feeling faint," I say,

pretending to swoon. "I'm such a delicate flower."

"My ass," Rollins says, nudging me with his elbow. "You're about as delicate as an AK-47." His snicker fades as he catches sight of my forehead. "Seriously, though, what happened?"

I shake my pink hair so it covers my wound. "It's nothing. I just passed out in the bathroom. But I'm fine. No big deal."

Rollins can't hide his worries, though he tries. His eyes narrow. "If you say so."

I squirm. Concern makes me itchy.

"Look, I gotta get to class. See you later?"

Rollins nods. "Later, Vee."

When I get back to English, it looks like someone released sleeping gas in the classroom. Almost everyone is draped over their desks, holding their copies of *Julius Caesar* at odd angles in front of their faces so it's not completely obvious they're asleep. Mrs. Winger is still absorbed in her game. She doesn't look up when I ease into my seat.

Samantha Phillips, her hair framing her face in straight red sheets, eyeballs me from across the room. Her cheerleading skirt is yanked up to show off her fake-baked thighs. I can't believe I once wore one of those skirts. I can't believe I was ever friends with the girl who is now captain of the squad. Sophomore year seems like a lifetime ago.

She looks at my Oasis T-shirt and sneers. "Nice outfit. What is it, like, 1994?"

I give her a death glare until she looks away and goes back to inconspicuously tapping buttons on her iPhone.

My gaze falls on the crisp, clean copy of *Astronomy: The Cosmic Perspective*, which peeks out from my black schoolbag. I had to order it brand-new to avoid the possibility of sliding when I flipped through the pages. People have emotional ties with books more often than you think, and I try to play it safe.

With Mrs. Winger so enthralled by her computer game, it would be easy to pull my book out and continue the section on black holes I was reading the night before. There probably won't be any questions about black holes on the *Julius Caesar* test, though, sadly enough.

I turn to Icky. "What'd I miss?"

"Hmmm . . . Well, the conspirators stabbed Caesar. You missed about the only good part in this play."

"Aw, crap," I say in mock annoyance. I lean over his desk, careful not to touch the book, and scan the part I missed. Yada yada yada, the conspirators surround him, Caesar is history.

One of the questions on the study guide: What were Caesar's last words?

I look back at the book, searching for the answer. Aha! Right after Brutus plunges the knife in, Caesar says, "*Et tu, Brute?*—Then fall, Caesar."

I think of Caesar going to the Capitol, surrounded by men he thought were his friends, only to be stabbed repeatedly in the back. And there's Brutus, holding the bloody freaking knife. The only thing left for Caesar to do is die, thinking he's such a shitty person even his best friend wants him dead.

Sophie's face pops into my head. What will she think when she finds out her two best friends are plotting against her? On her birthday, no less?

People suck.

I shake my head, writing down the answer.

"Pretty sick stuff, eh?" Icky grins.

"I'll say."

The bell rings, and everyone jumps to life.

Lunchtime.

I sit in my usual place, underneath the bleachers, and wait for Rollins. From my spot, I spy an empty Coke can, half a Snickers bar, and a Trojan wrapper. Fumbling in my backpack for my lunch, I wonder who in their right mind would want to have sex under the bleachers. Maybe they did it on the football field and the wrapper just blew over here—not that that's much better.

The brown sugar Pop-Tarts I packed this morning have crumbled to bits, so I eat the big pieces and then tilt my head back and dump the rest of the crumbs into my mouth.

I expect Rollins to sneak up on me and make a snarky comment about my ladylike table manners, but he doesn't show. This is the third lunch he's stood me up for. After a few minutes, I pull out my astronomy book and read about black holes in between swigs of warm Mountain Dew.

I'm in the middle of a really great paragraph about

how nothing—not even light—can escape a black hole once it's reached the event horizon when something above me clangs. Two people are working their way down the bleachers. I stick my finger in the book to hold my place and tilt my head up, annoyed by the interruption.

A familiar voice floats down to where I'm sitting. It makes me want to puke.

Scotch.

They sit down above me, and I hear another guy's voice. "Dude, you have to check this out." His tone is conspiratorial, like he's got some drugs or a *Penthouse* magazine.

Quietly, I stuff my book into my backpack. Maybe I can sneak away without them noticing me.

"What is this? Where did you get this?" I hear Scotch ask.

"One of the cheerleaders sent it out this morning. Hey. Didn't you bang this chick?"

Scotch snorts. "Yeah, once."

Feeling like I'm going to be sick, I crawl toward the opening beneath the bleachers. Something sharp slices into my knee, and it takes everything in me to stifle my yelp of pain. When I look down, I realize I've cut myself on a broken Budweiser bottle. My jeans are torn, and blood oozes through the opening. I bite my lip and move toward the exit.

After emerging from my hiding spot, I risk one quick backward glance. Scotch and another football player are both staring down at a cell phone, smirking. My heart clenches for the poor girl they're discussing, whoever she is.

In the bathroom, I clutch a wad of paper towels to my knee, but the blood doesn't seem to be slowing. Though I've been avoiding the school nurse, it's clear I'll have to stop by her office. The beer bottle wasn't exactly clean, and she'll have some antiseptic cream to smooth on the wound.

Mrs. Price is sitting at her desk, rifling through papers, when I arrive. Her gray hair is falling out of a loose bun, and she's wearing these glasses on a chain that make her look more like a librarian than a school nurse. She's so engrossed in her work, she doesn't even notice me come in.

A boy I've never seen before sits in a folding chair in the corner. He looks me up and down, his gaze pausing on the bloody paper towels I'm holding, making me feel suddenly self-conscious. He doesn't look like the type of guy who goes for chicks with pink hair. In fact, with his perfectly tousled blond hair and green T-shirt stretched tight over his biceps, he looks like the type of guy who dates girls who resemble Victoria's Secret models. Still, he sits there smiling as if he knows me or something.

"Uh," I say.

Mrs. Price looks up, her eyebrows jumping when she spots the blood. "Vee! Another accident?"

"No biggie," I mutter, avoiding eye contact with the guy. "It's a shallow cut. Just needs to be cleaned."

Mrs. Price frowns and pushes back her chair. She glides over to me and stoops down to examine my wound. "Did you get this during another episode, Vee?"

"No," I say, shaking my hair over my face so she won't notice the bump. If she realizes I've been passing out, she'll have to call my father and he'll have to call my doctors and they'll ask about the Provigil and the whole thing will be a big pain in my ass.

Mrs. Price snaps on some latex gloves and tells me to sit down and pull up my pant leg. She wipes my knee with an alcohol pad, dabs on some Neosporin, and then wraps it with a clean bandage. The whole time, I am intensely aware of the hot guy staring at my bare leg.

Mrs. Price strips off her gloves and tosses them into the trash. She stands and turns to the guy. "All your records seem to be in order, Zane. What class do you have now? Vee here can show you the way. Sylvia, this is Zane Huxley. This is his first day."

The guy steps forward and shakes my hand. "Nice to meet you." He pulls a crinkled paper from his pocket and squints at it. "I've got AP psych with Golden."

"Oh, good." Mrs. Price claps her hands. "That's where you're going. Right, Vee?"

"Um, yeah."

As we walk to Mr. Golden's room, I keep my eyes straight ahead, though I can feel Zane's eyes on me.

"So, Sylvia. Got any advice for the newb in town? Cool places to hang out? Teachers to avoid?" He reaches out and trails his finger along a poster that says STAR in bubble letters. Safe, Tolerant, Accountable, Respectful—all the things teachers wish students were, but we can't always be because we're human beings and not robots.

"Not really. Get salad bar on Chef's Choice days."

He laughs. "Well, that's a given." He unfolds his schedule. "I've got Winger first period. Have you had her?"

I risk a glance at Zane. His face is open and friendly and interested. To him, I'm a perfectly normal girl. Well, a perfectly normal girl with Pepto-colored hair. But still.

"Yeah. Actually, I've got her first period, too. Just don't bother her when she's playing solitaire, and you should be fine. She gets cranky."

"Solitaire, eh? What about this guy? Golden? He cool?"

"Yeah, he's really cool," I say. "He's young, which means he hasn't burned out yet. And he always tells these weird stories, like the time he helped a woman give birth at the Omaha zoo."

"Ew," Zane says, but he looks fascinated.

"Yeah. So where are you from?"

A girl in a flippy skirt skips down the hall toward us, her eyes lingering on Zane, but he doesn't even look her way. His eyes are fixed on me.

"Actually, I used to live here when I was little. But then my dad died and we moved to Chicago to live with my grandma."

Awkward. It's always so *awkward* when someone mentions death, especially when you don't know them very well. Strangers always say they're soooooo sorry when they hear my mother is gone, but it's wrong that death is a loss. It's something you gain. Death is always there, whispering in your ear. In your memories. In everything you think and say and feel and wish. It's always there.

I know there's nothing you can say to make death okay. It is what it is.

"That sucks," I say.

He nods silently.

We're standing in front of the door to Mr. Golden's classroom.

"Well, here we are," I say feebly.

"Try to contain your excitement," he says, smiling as he pushes open the door.

The room we walk into looks more like a lounge than a classroom. Mr. Golden likes to rescue and reupholster couches and bring them in for us to sit on during class discussions. He's decorated the walls with seemingly no rhyme or reason. Mixed in with the posters of Freud and diagrams of the human brain are old concert posters for The Doors and Jimi Hendrix. He even has a black light he turns on for special occasions. A large green plant that looks like it could swallow me hulks in the corner.

"Looks like we have a newcomer," Mr. Golden booms. "Take a seat wherever. I'm not into seating charts."

Zane folds himself into a beanbag chair. He's so tall, his knees almost hit his chin. The girls who aren't sneaking looks at him are openly gaping. A little seed of pleasure bursts within me when he looks my way and grins.

Rollins sits on an orange sofa in the corner, doodling in the margin of his textbook. I plop down next to him and pull out my notebook. Mr. Golden may let us sit wherever we want, but he draws heavily from his lectures when writing his exams. I got a C on the last one, so I figure I'd better actually try to follow what Mr. Golden is saying about classical conditioning.

"Who's that?" Rollins asks under his breath, nodding in Zane's direction. Rollins doesn't bother to take notes. He's got some kind of photographic memory; he remembers not only what he sees, but also what he reads, hears, and even smells. Ask him what was for lunch last Tuesday, and he'll remember just how nasty the burned meatloaf smelled in the hallways.

"Uh, Zane Huxley," I whisper back when Mr. Golden pauses to blow his nose. "He's new. I met him in the nurse's office. Sliced my knee open pretty good."

Rollins's eyes dart down to my leg. "You okay?"

"Yeah, yeah, I'm fine. I just kneeled on a beer bottle under the bleachers. No. Big. Deal. Anyway, where were you during lunch?"

Rollins pauses before answering. I can tell he knows there's more to the story, but I don't want to rehash the conversation I overheard under the bleachers. It's just too depressing.

He tugs his lip ring. "I was printing off the latest installment of *Fear and Loathing in High School*. My finest work, if I do say so myself." Pride creeps into his voice. Rollins makes his own zine, in which he reviews concerts and writes articles about the suckiness that is high school. It's completely do-it-yourself, literally cut and pasted from Rollins's journals and drawings.

"Ooooh, can I have one?"

"They're in my locker. I'll give you one later."

Mr. Golden launches back into his lecture. By the end of the period, I've covered a whole page with my loopy handwriting.

When the bell rings, Mr. Golden raises his voice. "Remember to read the section on the different theories of motivation tonight. There might be a quiz Monday, just so you know."

I'm stuffing my notebook back into my backpack when Mr. Golden turns to address me.

"Sylvia, can I speak with you for a moment?"

Rollins pokes me in the back. "See you later."

When we're alone, Mr. Golden perches on a sofa and crosses his arms over his chest. I hover in the middle of the room, wondering what he could possibly want with me. I'm pulling an overall B in his class, despite the C I received on the last exam. I would be an utterly unremarkable student if it weren't for my so-called narcolepsy.

"Sylvia, is everything okay?" he asks, his voice full of concern.

"Yeah," I say, racking my brain for any reason for him to think things are not okay. I must be sending out some really *not okay* vibes today. "Why?"

"It's just that I noticed you got a C on the test last week. The work you turned in prior to that test was of much higher quality. I don't mean to pry, but is there something wrong? Did you not study for the test?"

If I wanted to, I could probably play the narcolepsy card and say I wasn't able to concentrate on my studies. *I've*

been having such a rough time, I tried my best, really I did . . .
but that would be a lie. And there's something about Mr.
Golden that makes me want to be honest with him.

"Sorry, Mr. Golden. Guess I just forgot to study. I'll
try harder."

He leans forward and lowers his voice. "Listen, Sylvia,
if you ever need some extra help, I'd be happy to oblige.
Why don't you come in after school some day?"

I look down and shuffle my feet, trying to think of a
polite way to say I don't really need his help—the problem was that I didn't open my psychology book for like
a month.

"Oh, um. Thanks, Mr. Golden. I'm usually pretty busy
after school, though. I'm sure I'll do better on the next test
if I just study a little more."

Mr. Golden straightens up. "Well, just keep it in mind.
I'm here for you, after all."

I smile and nod before turning to leave. He follows me
to the door and closes it behind me with a firm *click*.

CHAPTER THREE

After school, Rollins stands waiting at my locker, holding a stack of xeroxed booklets.

"So what did Goldy want?"

"Oh," I say, waving my hand. "He just wanted to know why I'm such a slacker. I told him I'm naturally lazy. Can I have one?" I gesture to the zines.

He pulls out a copy wrapped in plastic. "I know what a germaphobe you are," he says teasingly. That's Rollins's explanation for why I don't like to touch things other people have handled—I'm totally OCD.

I unwrap the zine and examine it. On the cover it says *Fear and Loathing in High School No. 7*. There's a hand-drawn picture of a grotesque dog making its way down a hall lined with lockers, bags of weed and capsules hanging from its drooling jaws—a reference to Jimmy Pine's arrest, I'm guessing.

"Nice artwork," I say, admiring the cover.

He does all the drawing and writing in Sharpie, then goes to Copyworld to make dozens of copies. Every couple of months he comes out with a new issue. He sells them for a dollar apiece at the record store where he works, Eternally Vinyl, but more often than not he hands them out for free. Sometimes he rides the bus and sneaks them into people's bags or pockets.

Looking over the table of contents, I see there's an article about how the administration had no right to search Jimmy Pine's locker without a warrant; a concert review for a local band, Who Killed My Sea Monkeys; and an article about the hypocrisy of the kids in Wise Choices, the student group against substance abuse.

I turn to page five and scan the article entitled "Dumb Choices: East High's Goody-Goodies Exposed." Rollins cut out Samantha Phillips's yearbook picture from last year and drew a beer can in one hand and a joint in the other. Samantha, along with being head cheerleader, is also the president of Wise Choices. I'm sure it's only for her college applications—or to throw her parents off her boozehound trail. She's been drinking wine coolers since middle school.

"We on for tonight?" Rollins stuffs the remaining zines into his backpack and zips it up, looking at me expectantly.

"Damn straight," I say, trying to hide the surprise in my voice. It's been our tradition to watch horror movies and order pizza on Friday nights, but he hasn't made it the last two weeks. "It's Friday Night Fright, isn't it?"

I'm trying to decide what I'm in the mood for—*The Ring* or *The Exorcist*—when I remember that Mattie's invited Amber over tonight. Shit. I'm so not in the mood to babysit a couple of cheerleaders.

"Hey, Amber Prescott is spending the night at my place tonight. Can we go to your house instead?" I mentally cross my fingers, already knowing what his answer will be, but hoping I'm wrong.

Panic rolls over Rollins's face, then disappears, so quickly I'm not even sure I saw it. "Uh, my mom's . . . painting the living room. The place is a mess. Drop cloths everywhere. Sorry."

Since I've known him, Rollins has never asked me over to his house. Every time I suggest a visit, he makes up some excuse about his mom redoing the bathroom or putting in new cabinets or something. By now, his house must be a freaking palace, with all the remodeling they've done. I'm pretty sure his mom is really an alkie or a hoarder or something.

I shrug. "That's okay. We'll just banish Mattie to her room."

His lips curl into a grin. "I'll see you tonight then." He slings his backpack over one shoulder and walks away.

After transferring some textbooks to my backpack, I slam my locker door and spin the knob. A couple of girls I used to be friends with pass me, whispering and giggling. They're not laughing at me, though. They don't even look my way. It's like I'm a ghost to them, like I don't even exist. I watch them hurry away, probably to cheerleading practice. Sighing, I head in the opposite direction.

When I walk by Mr. Golden's room, I see something strange. A girl is sitting on a couch, and Mr. Golden is leaning over her. I can't see her face—only a bit of long, black hair. It sounds like she's sobbing. He looks over his shoulder and catches me peeking. Embarrassed, I look at the floor and bolt away.

I rush toward the exit, staring at my shoes and wondering what a crying girl is doing in Mr. Golden's room after school hours.

As I push open the door, I plow into someone entering the school. At first, all I see is green T-shirt. My cheeks become warm as I realize who I've almost knocked over on my mission to put distance between myself and Mr. Golden.

Zane beams down at me. "In a rush to start the weekend, eh?"

I return his smile. "Isn't everyone?"

"God, yes. My friends from Chicago are coming to see my new house, and we're going to a show. You doing anything fun this weekend?"

"Oh, you know, the usual—cow tipping," I say.

"Nice. Have fun with that. And try not to run anyone else over." He winks.

"Just try to stay out of my way," I toss back, grinning, and step out into the fading afternoon sunlight. The air smells of burning leaves. Only a few cars are left in the student parking lot. I wonder which car is Zane's as I pop my headphones into my ears and trudge toward the sidewalk.

As I walk home, my mind keeps returning to the scene in Mr. Golden's room. I wonder who that girl on the couch was and what happened to her to make her cry so hard.

———

A curious piece of paper is taped to our front door, flapping in the wind. As I get closer, I realize it's a little square from a desk calendar. I rip it off the door and carry it inside to examine more closely. The date is circled several times in red marker.

October 19—today's date.

Weird.

I remember Sophie in the bathroom earlier, saying Mattie must have forgotten her birthday. Is this Sophie's attempt to remind Mattie? It seems out of character, but the desperate way Sophie was talking makes me think she's not in the best frame of mind.

I stuff the paper into my back pocket. Sophie doesn't need to give Mattie and Amber any more ammunition. If she just leaves them alone for a little while, I know it'll all blow over. They'll find something else to fixate on. They'll be friends again in a week.

I stand there for a while, feeling the emptiness of the house down to my bones. Shadows stretch long across the floor. I hear nothing but the steady tick-tock of the grandfather clock in the living room. I am totally alone.

Mattie's at cheerleading practice. Dad's at the hospital. Mom is . . . Well, Mom hasn't been here for a long, long time.

Everything about our house is pretty much the same as it was five years ago, when my mom died of cancer. Same faded curtains with little red cherries on them. Same old yellow wallpaper. Same hardwood floor covered by an ancient red-and-gold rug. Same ornate silver mirror opposite the front door.

I step closer to the mirror. The girl I see looks wild with her bright-pink hair—rebellious and free. I wish I felt that way inside. I dyed my hair because I needed a drastic change from pale blond—my natural hair color is exactly the same shade as my mother's. I was tired of looking in the mirror every day and seeing her, missing her.

Dyeing my hair couldn't disguise the other parts of her that lived on in me, though. The way my laughter borders on cackling when I find something hilarious, just like hers did. The way my skin refuses to tan, no matter how many hours I spend in the sun.

And I know she had narcolepsy, too. I've inherited that unfortunate gene from her. I remember her falling asleep sometimes while watching television or during dinner. When she woke up, she'd have the strangest little smile. I'd give anything to know what happened to her while she was asleep. If she was like me. If she slid.

I don't remember the first time it happened, but it was after my mother's death. My father told me about walking into my room when I was twelve years old and finding me on the floor, unconscious. I was barely breathing. He couldn't wake me up. He rushed me to the emergency room, but no one could figure out what was wrong with me. Eventually, I just woke up and was fine, like nothing happened.

The doctors conducted test after test. Eventually, with a lack of any better explanation for my periodic bouts of unconsciousness, they diagnosed me with narcolepsy— apparently it can start around puberty. When I tried to tell my father what was *really* happening to me, he started sending me to a shrink—a woman with bright-red hair named Mrs. Moran. She said I was dealing with the pain of my mother's death by making up stories. Crying out for attention. My father thought that made sense.

So that's when I started lying.

As time went on, I just got used to it. And I started to learn the rules. Like one time during a field trip when I was thirteen. I'd worn Miss Ryan's sweater because the air had suddenly turned cold and I hadn't brought a jacket to school that day. She warned me not to spill anything on it because her grandmother had knitted it for her. One minute, I was walking through the museum, studying the paintings on the wall, and the next—I wasn't anymore.

I was back on the school bus. Suddenly a man came up behind me and circled his arm around my waist. He said, "Nancy, Nancy." Miss Ryan's first name. He spun me around, and I realized it was the bus driver.

He and his mustache came closer. His face descended onto mine, and his tongue went into my mouth. That was my first kiss. It was the most disgusting thing that had ever happened to me. It tasted like ashtrays and orange Tic Tacs. His hand slid under my blouse, and I prayed it would be over soon.

When I woke up, I was looking into a security guard's face. I'd fallen down and hit my head. He let me go when he was sure I didn't have a concussion or anything. I remember the moment when I handed Miss Ryan's fuzzy sweater back to her. Something just clicked. I realized my sliding into her had something to do with her sweater. She had left something of herself—her essence—on it, and I picked it up somehow. I wouldn't learn the word *empathy* until a couple of years later, but I understood the concept. It's seeing life through someone else's eyes. I had a gift.

Or a curse, depending on how you looked at it.

When I got onto the bus to go home, I couldn't help but stare at the driver. He winked at me, and I hurried past him. For years after, I had nightmares about him biting my face off.

At first, it didn't happen that often. Maybe every few months. But the uncertainty was enough to make me scared to touch anything. It was hard to tell which objects carried an emotional charge. There were the obvious things, the items people cherished and loved—like wedding rings or photos of grandparents—but there were unexpected things, too. A borrowed pencil. A library book. Anything someone was touching when they experienced an extreme emotion.

For a while, I wrapped my fingers with tape to keep myself from accidentally touching anything dangerous. But then I forgot and got sleepy and rested my cheek on a desk. I slid into an older boy stealing cigarettes from the grocery store. I felt his heart pounding beneath his big, black coat and the sweat under his arms. When my teacher woke me up, I stared into her face, terrified she'd know about the bad thing I'd just been doing.

But then I realized everyone was doing bad things. My teacher was sneaking drinks of liquid that made my throat burn. My sister was cheating during a math test. The mailman tucked packages into a special bag to take home. People were doing good things, too—writing thank-you notes, holding doors for old ladies, smiling at each other— but those people weren't the majority. The fact is that most people keep secrets hidden behind their eyes.

Lately, I've been sliding more often. Once a month turned into once a week and then a couple times a week. Now, even if I can manage a few days without sliding, I end up exhausted and unfocused and even more susceptible to the slides than usual. It's like the sliding is picking up momentum somehow. It's like there's a reason behind it. I just wish I knew what it was.

In my room, I throw my backpack onto my bed, but the stress doesn't ease from my shoulders. Something is weighing me down. Maybe it's the way those ugly words felt coming out of Amber's mouth. Maybe it's Sophie's desperation. Maybe it's how Zane's smile made me buzz like there's electricity coursing through my veins. I don't know exactly what it is, but I need something to help me unwind.

I need music.

In my closet, behind my mountain of Converse shoes in all the colors of the rainbow, I keep a box of my mother's CDs. I don't know why I hide them; my dad doesn't care that I have them, and my sister couldn't be less interested in music from the nineties, but it's like, if I keep them packed away, they'll stay fresh—they'll keep my mother with me just a little longer.

I push a Pearl Jam CD into my laptop and then crawl onto my bed. I retrieve the astronomy book and run my fingers over the cover. It's black, sprinkled with peepholes of light. There's nothing as gorgeous as the night sky. Nothing.

Flipping through the pages, I find the corner I carefully turned down to mark my place. Black holes. They're so intense and sad. When massive stars die, their cores grow so dense with gravity that they pull other things in, suck them into infinity. Black holes seem impossible, like they defy the laws of physics, but there it all is, in black-and-white. I wish there were a textbook that would explain the phenomena of sliding to me.

The song "Alive" comes on, and my heart trips a little. I lean back against my pillow and listen to the words. I think it's about this kid finding out his father is dead. Even though the kid never knew his father, the death leaves a scar on him. An absence so all-encompassing, it's there even in his happiest moments.

I close my eyes and wish I could tell my mother about my day. I'd tell her I'm worried about Sophie and how there's a new boy who's really kind of hot and how I think Mattie and Amber are up to no good. I'd tell her I miss her. I'd tell her I love her. I'd tell her everything.

CHAPTER FOUR

A couple of hours later, Mattie and Amber spill into the kitchen, all ponytails and giggles and pom-poms. I roll my eyes over my glass of chocolate milk. Through the kitchen window, I see Samantha Phillips's car pull away from the curb. The ridiculous thing is that, instead of just ditching me as a friend, Samantha hangs out with my little sister now, like she's upgraded to a newer, shinier version of me. I suppose it was inevitable, since Mattie joined the cheerleading squad. And Mattie has way more in common with her than I ever did. I've heard Mattie spend hours on the phone with Samantha, debating the merits of thong underwear.

Mattie tosses her purse and pom-poms onto the kitchen table before raiding the fridge. "Hey!" She grimaces at me. "You finished the chocolate milk."

She pulls out a bottle of Evian and twists the cap off before taking a long gulp.

Amber helps herself to a bottle of water and shakes it at my sister. "You don't need chocolate milk, anyway, honey.

Remember, we're off sugar and flour."

Mattie sticks out her tongue at Amber.

"So, what are the chances I can get you guys to lie low tonight?" I hoist myself onto the kitchen counter. "Rollins is coming over to watch movies."

At the mention of Rollins's name, Amber stands up straight. I can practically smell the pheromones coming off her.

"What will you give us to stay in my room?" Mattie, ever the negotiator, asks. Her gaze drifts up to the half-empty bottle of Captain Morgan on top of the refrigerator.

"There's loads of sugar in rum," I say, unable to keep the irritation out of my voice.

"Booze doesn't count," Amber announces. "Your body burns booze calories superquick. Especially if we practice our new routine a few times." She swivels her hips and tosses her ponytail in either an epileptic seizure or their new routine.

"Please?" Mattie's eyes are pleading. "We'll just stay in my room. Won't we, Amber?"

Amber shrugs. "Whatever."

I sigh. If they actually stay in Mattie's room, I'll be free to enjoy the movie instead of having to explain the plot to Mattie, and Rollins won't have a freshman in heat crawling all over his lap. Besides, if I tell them no, they'll just sneak it anyway. Isn't it better that they drink here, where I can keep an eye on them?

"Fine," I say. "Just stay in your room."

"Yoink!" Mattie grabs the bottle of rum.

Amber paws through the refrigerator until she finds a two-liter of Coke. "Don't you have any Diet?" she whines, and I shoot her death rays until she looks away.

Armed with booze, Coke, glasses, ice, and a butter knife to mix their drinks, the girls bounce out of the kitchen and up the stairs. Just in time, too. At that moment, Rollins pulls up in his old Nissan Stanza.

I watch him climb out of the car and amble up the front walk, carrying something under his arm. He runs his fingers through his hair before ringing the doorbell. When I open the door, he holds his hands behind his back.

"Choose," he says.

"Choose what?"

"Choose a hand. Right or left."

I point at his right hand, and he brings it forward. I've chosen *The Exorcist*.

"Wise choice." He nods.

"Mos def," I say. "What's in the other hand?"

He slowly reveals his other hand. He's clutching a bundle of blue cloth. He shakes it out, and I see that it's a T-shirt. I suck in my breath. The cover of The Smashing Pumpkins' album *Mellon Collie and the Infinite Sadness*, with an angel bursting out of a star, is on the front. *Mellon Collie* is one of my favorite albums. I've been trolling eBay for this shirt for ages.

"It came in with a shipment of vintage T-shirts," Rollins says. "Is it the right one?"

"OhmyGod!" I cry, jumping up and down. "I've been looking for this *forever*."

Rollins laughs at my excitement. "Are you sure? I can take it back if you don't like it. . . ." He playfully tugs it away from me, and I slap his hand.

Rollins follows me into the living room and flops onto our plaid couch, in his regular spot. I lay the T-shirt carefully over the top of the couch, a cheesy smile plastered on my face, and pop the DVD into the player before throwing myself into the recliner.

"So who's your dad operating on today?"

"Ah, I forgot to tell you. Conjoined twins."

Rollins's eyebrows jump with interest. "Really? Conjoined twins? Awesome."

I knew he'd be excited at the prospect of real, live conjoined twins. There was one time last year when we were so bored that we went to Goodwill and bought a size XXXL shirt we could both fit into. We went to the mall, and everyone stared at us while we fed each other sticky buns and went up and down the escalator. Rollins even accompanied me into the girls' bathroom and looked away while I peed. I know it wouldn't be fun to *really* be a conjoined twin, but we love the concept of it.

I fill him in on the details of the operation. In a weird way, I envy the soon-to-be-separated twins—assuming everything goes well. Soon they will be nestled in their bassinettes, able to lead normal, uncomplicated lives. I wish there was an operation my dad could do to fix whatever is wrong with me.

"That's intense. It's so cool that your dad is able to

have that kind of impact," Rollins says, pulling a loose string off his T-shirt.

"Jared Bell saves the day again," I say.

I'm unable to stop the dark feeling that passes through me. Yeah, my dad has a positive effect on so many lives—just not mine. Maybe if I saw him more than a few minutes a day, *if that*. I immediately feel terrible for the thought. Selfish. Sick babies are way more important than my getting to hang out with my dad. He's a hero for being able to put right what nature made wrong.

I aim the remote control toward the DVD player to start the movie. The sky is just beginning to darken into night. Rollins interrupts the movie every few minutes with a snarky comment. I pull a quilt tight around me, wrapping myself in the moment, the familiarity. This is the way our friendship used to be, before we started drifting apart. I miss it.

Linda Blair's head is just about to start spinning like a top full of vomit when Mattie bursts into the living room, followed by Amber. Mattie bumps into the coffee table and giggles. Someone's been hitting the rum a little too hard.

"Oh, *hello*, lovely sister. So sorry to bother you. But Samantha's coming to pick us up, and we're going to a movie." She slurs her words slightly and laughs again.

Amber eyes Rollins hungrily. She plops down next to him on the couch and gives him a sly smile. The tiniest worm of envy works its way through the apple of my heart. I don't know where it comes from, but it annoys me and I squash it by glaring at my sister.

"Mattie," I growl. "You said you were going to stay here tonight." My eyes gravitate toward Amber and Rollins on the couch. She's batting her eyes at him, and it looks like he's trying to inch away from her.

"Come on, Vee. All the Poms are going to be there. Do you want me to miss out?" She yanks up the volume on her "poor me" shtick, the one I always fall for.

Out of the corner of my eye, I see Amber moving closer to Rollins and hitching up her skirt. She lifts a single finger and reaches out to touch Rollins's pierced lip. "I like your piercing. I bet it feels great—"

I interrupt Amber. "Fine, Mattie. Go to the movie. But you'd better be back here by midnight."

A blaring comes from outside, probably Samantha leaning on her horn.

Mattie whoops. "Come on, Amber, let's go." She pries Amber away from Rollins, and the two of them skip out the door.

The older-sister part of me winces at the thought of letting Mattie go out, as drunk as she is, but the rest of me feels suddenly lightened. At least they're gone. They're Samantha's problem now. And why do I always have to be the teenybopper police, anyway? I'm not the parent. I deserve a night to just enjoy myself, don't I?

Rollins looks relieved, too. "Should we rewind? We missed the best part." It takes me a moment to realize Rollins is talking about the movie.

"Oh, yeah." I find the remote control under a pillow on the floor. After locating the part we were watching before we were so rudely interrupted, I push Play.

I settle back into the chair and pull the blanket up to my chin. After a while, my eyelids start to droop. I shake my head, trying to wake myself up.

"Vee? Are you okay?"

I hold up a finger and take deep breaths, but it does no good. I feel that I'm about to go. Quickly, I take inventory of what I'm touching. Chair, blanket, clothes. So I could slide into anyone who's sat in this chair recently—my dad or Mattie. Shit.

I jump out of the chair, not wanting to slide into my father in the middle of some gross medical procedure, but it's too late. I feel myself falling to the floor. Rollins cries out.

Wherever I am, it's not the hospital. I'm not at the movie theater, either. I'm in a bedroom—a girl's bedroom, it looks like.

The girl I've become cries as though someone ripped her heart in half. She sobs, clutching a lacy blanket, wiping snot on it. Someone rubs her back. The pressure against her skin moves in circles, this way and that. It feels so good. It feels like everything I should have but don't.

The sensation calms me, but it does nothing to stop the noise coming out of the girl I've slipped into. She wails like a banshee for ten seconds, then gulps in air until it feels like her lungs are going to explode. The pink walls, punctuated with framed pictures of ballerinas, seem to be closing in.

A middle-aged woman, presumably the back-rubber, comes into view. Her cheeks are full and flushed, and she reaches out a soft hand to tousle the girl's hair.

This is what a mother is.

"Honey, those girls are no good for you. I've been telling you that all along."

The girl just cries harder. I can barely see through her tears.

"Sophie," the woman says.

The realization creeps up on me: I'm inside Sophie Jacobs. What could I have been touching that would have Sophie's imprint on it? I suppose she's been over at our house enough times. She's probably sat in that recliner.

The scene in the locker room this morning comes rushing back to me. Amber and Mattie. Who else could "those girls" be? They betrayed her somehow, went forward with their plan to "put her in her place." But how? What did they *do* to her?

"I don't understand," Sophie says. "How could they be so mean? They're supposed to be my *friends*." She wipes her eyes with the comforter, clearing my vision for the moment. Her mother hovers inches away. She hooks one finger under Sophie's chin and tilts her head up, looks her straight in the eye.

"Sophie, listen to me. True friends would never do what they did to you. Do you understand me? And on your birthday, no less. What kind of monsters do that? The best thing you can do is cut them loose. Be strong. You'll be so much better off."

What did they do? What did Mattie and Amber do that was so terrible?

Sophie sputters. "Mom. I'm not strong. I'm not."

An image slices through my mind: Sophie, on her hands and knees in the bathroom. I wonder if that's what Sophie's thinking of. I wish I could reach in, pull out her thoughts, examine them like a roll of film. But I don't have that kind of power. I am only a passenger. A witness.

Sophie's mother speaks firmly. "You're stronger than you'll ever know."

Sophie's breath gradually becomes more even. Her mother holds out her hands, and Sophie grasps them. They feel soft. I don't want to like it so much, this feeling of a mother. I don't want to know what I'm missing.

"Come on. Let's go have some chocolate-chip ice cream. Don't think I haven't noticed how skinny you've been getting."

Sophie tenses. Again, I remember Sophie curved around the toilet. Something within her breaks. Her body relaxes, her decision made. She lets her mother lead her out of the room.

"Sylvia?"

Rollins's face is inches from my own. I'm sprawled on the floor, and he's leaning over me, his brow furrowed. He pulls me into a sitting position, and his fingers catch on something around my wrist.

Sophie's bracelet, meant for Mattie. That's what made me slide. She must have imprinted on it while she was braiding it. I slip it off and toss it onto the coffee table.

"What's that? You joining the cheerleading squad?"

I rub my temples. "Ugh. No. That's for Mattie. Argh. My head."

Rollins rubs my shoulder sympathetically. "Twice in one day. You must be exhausted."

"Yeah." I sigh. A part of me, small but growing every day, wants to come clean to Rollins. I mean, Rollins knows everything about me. Everything but *that*. Rollins is ruled by logic, though. If I told him I slid into other people's minds, he'd laugh at me.

Wouldn't he?

Peering into his brown eyes, I wonder if I've misjudged him. Maybe I could tell him. Maybe I could make him understand.

"Would it sound crazy if . . ." I trail off, not sure where to go from there. I remember my father's expression when I told him about sliding—as if I'd just said an alien had visited me in the night.

"I'm sorry," I say, pulling away from him. "Really. I'm fine."

Rollins looks disappointed. I feel like I've let him down. I know he wants me to open up, confide in him—but I can't. I just can't.

"I should go," he says. He grabs his leather jacket off the back of the couch. I follow him out of the living room and into the darkness of the front entryway, my mouth opening and closing like a fish's. I'm afraid this is it—if he leaves now, our friendship will never go back to normal. I want to say *stop*. I want to say *stay*, but nothing comes out.

We stand near the door. Rollins's face softens for a split second, and he reaches out and gently brushes my hair back, revealing the bump on my forehead. I don't like the way it feels, so exposed. Wincing, I push his hand away.

He shakes his head and turns to open the door.

"See you later," he says, his jaw firm, and he disappears into the crisp night air. After a moment, his car flares to life and roars away. I stand there, watching his taillights get smaller and smaller. There's a bitter taste in my mouth. Finally, I hit the switch for the porch light so my sister will be able to see when she gets home.

CHAPTER FIVE

I wander into the middle of my room and just stand there for a minute, not knowing what to do with myself. There's something about being alone on a Friday night—it's more lonely than any other night, I think. It's like my loserishness has been highlighted by the simple fact that I'm standing here by myself at nine p.m. on a Friday.

I have to put on some Weezer to make the space a little less quiet. I stare at the walls, at the Nine Inch Nails and Green Day posters hanging over my bed. They remind me of Rollins—he'd call me every time something he thought I'd like came in. "You and your old nineties music," he'd say, grinning, shaking his head.

The way he walked out tonight, though—it makes me scared I've lost him for good. I've shut down his every attempt to find out what's really going on with me. I know what Dr. Moran would say—I'm pushing him away before he has a chance to disappoint me.

I try to find something in my room from before we were friends, a hint at what my life used to be like, but there's nothing. Finally, I turn to my closet. I push aside the clothes I wear every day and peek in the back. It's like a time capsule—my old cheerleading uniform, the preppy sweaters I used to wear when I hung out with Samantha.

When my fingers hook the glittery purple gown I wore to homecoming last year, I yank my hand back as if from a cobra. The poisonous memories come rushing back.

On the first day of sophomore year, I felt this heady rush of possibility. Cheerleading tryouts were coming up, and Samantha and I pinkie-swore we'd get on the squad. When we did, we celebrated by sneaking wine coolers from her older brother's fridge.

My locker was right next to Scott Becker's—before people started calling him Scotch. Samantha and I both had the hots for him. He was smaller then, with sandy-blond hair and dimples. He did this thing where he'd stare at me until I looked, and then he'd get all red and turn his gaze to the floor.

On the last Friday in September, he asked me to go to the homecoming dance with him. I thought Samantha would be excited for me. Okay, that's bullshit. I knew she'd be pissed. But I said yes anyway.

If I could take back anything that happened in my life—well, besides my mother dying, of course—it would be saying yes to Scott Becker.

Samantha turned mean, getting the rest of the cheer-leaders to turn against me. In health class, we did these PowerPoint presentations on sexually transmitted diseases. Samantha's was about herpes, and she Photoshopped my head onto a purple dinosaur and called it the Herpasaurus Rex. Everyone laughed, including the teacher.

Samantha spread a rumor that I gave head to all the seniors on the football team. My phone number was in every stall in the boys' bathroom. Saturday mornings, our trees were full of toilet paper.

Whenever a cheerleader cupped her hand around someone's ear and whispered a secret, all the while staring at me, I felt like dying. But to give in would be to let them win, and there was no way I was going to do that. I tried to make it seem like the rumors didn't bother me. Like I didn't care.

Only at night, when sleep was impossible, did I cry.

The weekend before homecoming, my dad took Mattie and me to the mall to look for a dress. He pressed a few bills, crisp from the ATM, into my hand and headed for the food court. Mattie pirouetted and skipped by my side, but it wasn't all fun and frills for me. It was war.

I wanted a dress that would stun, that would show everyone how little I thought of the rumors and pranks. It needed to bring the boys to their knees and the girls to their senses. It needed to double as armor.

At one end of the mall, next to Pretzels 'n' More, we found a store called Tonight, Tonight. The dress jumped out at me from the window—a dark-purple, silky, sparkly thing. It reminded me of the stream in the woods behind our house, of water spilling over rocks and twinkling in the moonlight.

When I put it on, I felt strong in a way I'd never felt before. I felt like someone else, someone older and wiser, someone who knew what she wanted out of life. The front came down dangerously low, skimming the tops of my barely-there breasts, but the saleslady pulled out these chicken-cutlet things and stuffed them in my bra, and it was like I had *bloomed*.

When we got home, I tried my dress on and sashayed down the stairs like a princess. I could tell my dad wasn't too crazy about the dress and the chicken-cutlet things, but he said, "I guess you're old enough to pick your own clothes" and "You only go to your first high school dance once" and "You sort of look like your mother in that thing"—and then he stopped talking and went into his study.

A guy on the football team with a goatee drove us to the dance, but first he took us to Kapler Park and pulled out a joint. I said no to the pot, but I took a few swigs from the bottle of Cutty Sark that Scott had lifted from his parents' liquor cabinet. It made me feel the way the dress did— warm and grown-up and free. When we all felt light and fuzzy, we headed to the dance. It occurred to me that the goatee guy probably shouldn't be driving, but the liquor made me feel like nothing bad could really happen, and I didn't want to seem like a baby.

"Come dance with me," Scott whispered in my ear. I let him lead me out to the middle of the dance floor, and it seemed like the whole crowd parted to let us through, just like in a movie. A slow song played, and I leaned against him and closed my eyes. He smelled like pot and orange shampoo. It felt perfect. But then a familiar feeling crept over me—I was about to slide—and I mumbled to Scott that I needed to sit down.

"You want to go sit somewhere alone?"

I nodded and rubbed my eyes. I could barely stand up. By the time Scott maneuvered me to the edge of the gym, by the doors that led to the locker rooms, I'd already slid into someone else.

It was a strange feeling. I'd left my body, but I was still in the gym. It was just like my perspective had changed. The body I'd slid into was standing near the punch bowl, sipping sweet liquid out of a paper cup. Her beautiful pink ring flashed under the disco lights. That's when I realized who I'd slid into. I was wearing Samantha's silver heels, ones I'd borrowed long before our fight, ones that she'd said made her feel like Cinderella.

My ex-best friend watched Scott drag my body into the boys' locker room.

My worst fear was coming true. When you abandon your body, you leave it vulnerable. Maybe Scott was just looking for a place to sit with me and wait until I woke up, but then why didn't he just prop me up on one of the folding chairs set up along the perimeter of the gym? Or, better yet, why didn't he find a chaperone and ask for help?

I was pretty sure I knew why, but I couldn't stomach the reason. I couldn't think about what was happening to my body without me to protect it. I desperately wished I could force Samantha to follow Scott, to punch him in the mouth, or even just to scream for help. But there was nothing I could do.

After a few moments, I saw a boy with long brown hair and a lip piercing duck into the locker room. He was in my Spanish class—a new kid named Archie Rollins. Samantha and I had laughed out loud the first day Señora Gomez read roll call. Who names their son Archie?

My panic grew. I thought of a book I'd read about a girl who got wasted at a party. Some random guy took pictures of her naked body and posted them all over the internet. Everyone saw—even her parents.

Come on, Samantha, I thought. *I know we're in a fight, but how can you stand here and not do anything? How?*

That's when I returned.

I awoke to sounds of a scuffle. My body was laid out on one of those uncomfortable wooden benches in the boys' locker room, my dress around my waist. Two struggling figures became clearer until I figured out it was Scott and that guy, Archie.

Archie got a good punch in, and it caught Scott right under his chin. Scott's arms pinwheeled, searching for something to grab on to, but there was nothing. He fell hard on his back, groaning and looking like he wouldn't be getting up for a while.

Turning to me, Archie held out a hand. "Come on," he said, his voice gruff. "Let's get you out of here." I let him lead me out of the locker room, up the stairs, and outside into the cool night air. He folded me into his car, and I let him because I wasn't thinking about much of anything but how I needed a shower.

On Monday morning, I overheard a cheerleader whisper

to another sophomore that I'd gone down on Scott in the boys' locker room at the dance. "Who told you that?" the sophomore asked. "Samantha," the cheerleader responded, "so you know it's true. And then Scott yakked all over the dance floor." They giggled.

"Scotch Becker," they called him. To this day, he goes by a nickname he earned the night he tried to take advantage of me. Every time I hear it, I want to vomit.

After Spanish class, I confronted Samantha. "You saw it," I said. "You saw Scott dragging me into the locker room, but you just stood there and sipped your punch and didn't do *anything*." My voice was shaky, and I felt like I was going to cry, but I wouldn't give her the satisfaction.

Samantha stood with her folder clutched to her chest, her lips pressed together. In her eyes, I saw a mixture of anger, regret, and *fear*. I could tell she was wondering how I knew she saw it all when I was unconscious at the time. She was *afraid of me*, of what I knew and how I knew it. She turned and scuttled away.

When I got to lunch that day, Samantha was sitting on Scotch's lap. Everyone at their table followed me with their eyes as I grabbed a plate and filled it with some spinach leaves and croutons and ranch dressing. I sat at an empty table near the windows. That was when Archie—well, *Rollins*—sat down across from me. He had a bag of Doritos and a can of Mountain Dew. He looked at me easily, like there was nothing out of the ordinary, like he sat with me every day.

"What's up?" he asked, and we've been best friends ever since.

I didn't tell anyone what happened to me that night. Maybe I should have. *Probably* I should have. But I didn't, and even thinking about talking about it makes my skin crawl. It seems easier to pretend it never happened. The problem is . . . it *did* happen. And I carry it around with me every day of my life.

I don't even bother to undress, just lie on top of my covers, replaying my conversation with Rollins over and over again in my head, wishing it had gone a different way. What if I'd told Rollins the truth? What if he'd *believed* me? Does the fact that I couldn't be honest with Rollins mean I don't really value his friendship?

I sigh and turn onto my left side. The *A Clockwork Orange* poster on my wall is illuminated by the streetlight. I get into a staring contest with it, but it's no good. The eyeball with the thick black lashes always wins. I haul myself out of bed and pad across the room, to the window. My mother's old telescope waits for me.

She loved the stars. Even though she'd majored in English literature, my father said, she took so many classes in astronomy she was able to pick it up as a minor. Though so much about my mother seems intangible now—the way she smelled, the things she'd whisper before I fell asleep at night—*this* seems real to me. I'm able to look through her telescope and see exactly what she saw. It makes me feel close to her.

Stooping down, I look through the eyepiece. Despite the light pollution in our neighborhood, I'm able to make out Polaris, the North Star, and from that I'm able to identify Ursa Major and Ursa Minor. Mama bear and baby bear. There's something so comforting to me about the constellations, the mother and baby, cradled in the sky for all eternity. I stare until the stars go blurry and my breath goes soft.

Something in my pocket pokes me. I pull it out and smooth it against my jeans. It's the page from the calendar that Sophie taped to our door earlier. I start to feel woozy, like I might slide. *Oh no. Not again.* My vision pulses, and my knees go out, and I fall deep, deep down, into a hole.

I'm sitting at a white desk, a pad of fancy stationery angled before me. Words crawl like spiders across the page, flowing from the pen in my gloved hand.

Who am I?

And why am I wearing gloves?

The words I'm writing say: *I don't deserve this.*

As I stand, I notice the pink walls and the pictures of ballerinas. Sophie's room.

There is no sound.

I turn away from the desk, and I see the bed. It's definitely Sophie's bed, but it's a different color now. Earlier, the bed was covered with a pristine white comforter. Now, the bed is maroon. And wet. So wet. There's something on the bed. It is Sophie. Her inky-black hair frames her white face. Her arms lie helpless at her sides, a long slash in each wrist.

No.

No.

This isn't happening.

That's when I see what I'm holding in my gloved hands. A long, silver blade.

Oh. Shit. Oh. No.

Who did this to her? Who did I slide into?

But, before I can figure it out, I am gone.

My eyes fly open and I sit up, grabbing at my legs, my head, my face, to make sure I'm really back. The light from the streetlamp shines in my eyes, blinding me for a moment until I dodge out of the way. I pull myself to my feet and look around. Telescope, rocking chair, heap of dirty clothes. I'm back in my room.

What happened?

My eyes fall on the small piece of paper on the floor—the one I thought Sophie had taped to our door earlier. If she'd been the one to put it there, I would have slid into Sophie just now.

But I didn't.

I slid into someone else. Someone bad. Someone with a knife.

The memory of Sophie and her open wrists spurs me into action. I have to call, make sure she's okay. The only problem is that I don't have her number.

Mattie and Amber do.

I dash out the door and down the dark hallway to my sister's room. But no one's there. Her bed is empty, the wrinkled sheets nestled around no one. Mattie and Amber are still out.

I look at the clock. It's nearly midnight.

They should have been home by now if they were just going to a movie. As I return to my room to find my phone, I wonder what happened to them. Most likely they just crashed at Samantha's house for the night.

They're fine, I reassure myself. *Mattie is fine.*

I dial Mattie's number and wait. No answer. I dial again. No answer.

I make myself sit down and breathe. Just breathe.

For a moment, I think about calling my father. It's odd that he's not home by now. The only reason he'd still be at the hospital is if the conjoined twins are having problems, in which case I can't really call him up and bother him.

What do I do?

If I look up Sophie's home phone number, I can call her parents. My clock says 12:03. It's so late. They'll be angry.

Shaking my head, I realize that of course I have to call them. If what I saw was real, someone has to help Sophie. *Now.*

I fire up my laptop and type in Sophie's last name. Jacobs. There are six listings under that name in our area. I have no idea what her parents' names are. I'm going to have to try each of them.

I call the first number. No one picks up.

On my second try, a groggy-sounding woman answers.

"Is Sophie there?"

"You must have the wrong number," the woman says angrily, and hangs up.

Please let the third time be the charm. Please.

The phone rings.

"Hello?" a man asks cautiously.

"Is Sophie there?"

"She's asleep, like I was just a moment ago."

"Please, sir. Please go check on her."

"What is this about—"

"Please, I don't have time to explain. Please go check on her."

I hear the man set the phone down. A second passes, stretching out into forever. Another second. Another.

And then the screaming begins.

CHAPTER SIX

I sit up, groggy and confused. After swiping my hand over my eyes, it comes away smeared with black eye makeup.

My alarm clock says it's noon.

All at once, the night before rushes back to me like a bad dream. Blood on white sheets. Sophie's blood. The screams. The terrible screams.

The phone had gone dead after only about a minute, but I know the sounds of terror will live in me forever. I tried to call back several times, but the phone line was busy. Sophie's father must have hung up and called 911.

I'd sat up in bed for the longest time, chewing caffeine pills and waiting for Mattie and Amber to get home. I was determined not to close my eyes until I knew my sister was safe. But that's the thing about sleep—you can't avoid it forever. It waited until my defenses were down and sucked me under.

I trip over my blankets, racing to my sister's room. It's still empty. Where could she be?

I hear something down the hall—someone in the bathroom, retching into the toilet. I run to the door, try the knob, but it's locked. I bang on the door.

"Mattie!"

The noise stops long enough for the person in the bathroom to croak out a response. It's Amber. "Stop. Yelling. Mattie's in the kitchen."

My bare feet slap against the wooden steps as I run down to the kitchen. I have to find Mattie, have to tell her before she finds out on her own.

When I reach the kitchen, though, I see that I'm too late. Mattie is sitting on the floor, her back to the cabinets. Her skin is deathly pale. The mascara that's migrated to her cheeks looks like Japanese characters. She clutches her cell phone in a colorless hand.

"Mattie?" I say softly.

She shows no sign of hearing or understanding.

"Mattie." I sink down next to her on the yellow tile and wrap my arms around her. My touch seems to bring her to life, and she turns her head toward me.

"It's Sophie," she says. "She's dead."

Mattie trembles under my hug.

"She killed herself."

The night before washes over me, and I'm pulled back into the horror. I can see Sophie's wide, dead eyes. I remember the way the knife felt in my hand.

Sophie didn't kill herself.

She was murdered.

And I was there.

By the time I scrape Mattie off the kitchen floor and help her to her bedroom, Amber is gone, leaving behind only a small puddle of puke in the bathroom.

I tuck Mattie into bed, pull the covers up to her chin like I would for a child. She *is* a child, I have to remind myself. No matter how much rum she drinks or how short her skirts are or how she tells me to mind my own effing business, she is only a child. The evidence is everywhere— the unicorn collection on her shelf, the ballerina jewelry box on her bureau, the way she holds my hand and asks me not to leave. I tell her I'll only be gone a second, just long enough to call Dad and let him know what's going on, but she shakes until I give in and stay.

Around one, I hear the front door open. A breathy voice drifts down the hall, singing a pop song. Vanessa, our cleaning lady. She comes every Saturday to do the vacuuming and the scrubbing and the dusting.

"Knock, knock," she calls out, swinging open Mattie's door. She wears super-tight jeans and a low-cut black shirt, more appropriate for dancing at a club than cleaning a house. Her eyes widen in alarm when she spots Mattie in bed, looking positively terminal. "What happened?"

I rise and block Vanessa's view, mouthing, *Hangover.* Vanessa, still in college, nods in sympathy. She ducks back out of the room and shuts the door so softly I can barely hear the click.

When Mattie is finally snoring, I tiptoe out of the room and dial my father's number.

That night, Mattie and I sit on the stairs, waiting for the front door to open. Dad said he'd be home in an hour, but it's nearing dinnertime. Something must have gone wrong with the twins, to keep him away when something this major is going on.

Mattie leans her head against the wall. A photo in a silver frame hangs a foot above her head; in it, she and I are frozen in time—she is nine, and I am eleven. Between us, Mickey Mouse grins, but we cannot bring ourselves to smile. Our mother had died a month before. When my dad was going through the thickest stretch of his forest of grief, he sent us to Disney World with his parents. Why anyone wanted to document that trip, why he chose to hang this picture on the wall when we were so clearly a broken family, is anyone's guess. Maybe he needed to prove to himself that life does indeed go on, even after your wife dies, even after your children's mother is gone.

My left hand hovers over my sister's shoulder. I feel like I should rub her back the way Sophie's mother rubbed hers when she was upset, but I can't quite bring myself to do it. Something in the gesture would be false. I can't offer her the comfort she needs right now. In order to give something, you need to have it inside of you to give. And right now there's nothing inside me at all.

Nothing but the image of Sophie's dead body. It's all I can see. It's all I am.

All day, I've been picking up my cell phone, imagining myself dialing the number for the police station. But then I get stuck. I can't think of what I'd say. I can't think of how to explain.

I'm just about to get up and go into the kitchen to look for something to microwave for dinner when the door swings open. My dad stands in the doorway, a duffel bag slung over his trench coat and bags under his eyes.

"Daddy!" Mattie runs to him and hugs his thin frame tightly. He circles his arms around her, but there's a stiffness to his movement.

His eyes drift up to me. "I'm so sorry, girls. It was touch-and-go at the hospital. We thought one of the babies might have a blood clot. It was life-or-death."

"I'm going to see what's in the freezer," I announce, standing. I'm ashamed of the way I feel—resentful that those babies should take priority over us, his own flesh and blood.

"No, Vee. We need real food. I'll make something." He pulls back from Mattie gently.

"That's ridiculous, Dad. You're exhausted. I'll just make a frozen pizza."

He waves away my concern and grabs Mattie's hand, pulling her into the yellow light of the kitchen. "I'm fine."

I follow them, if only to make sure my father doesn't pass out standing up. Mattie takes one of the stools behind the counter, and I take the other. Together, we watch my father spin the knob on the oven and pull items out of the refrigerator: eggs, butter, an eggplant.

Watching him cook soothes me more than anything he could say. He guides a knife through the purple bulb with expert precision, cutting thin, even slices. Each egg makes a satisfying crack when he taps it against the sink. Each strip of eggplant is dipped in the egg mixture and then in bread crumbs and then laid carefully in a pan. Finally, he sprinkles flakes of cheese on top and slides the pan carefully into the oven.

Though my father has a recipe for my mother's famous eggplant parmesan in a bright-orange recipe book on the shelf above the sink, he's made it so many times he doesn't even need to look.

The recipe book, printed in my mother's own handwriting, has been a guide for him throughout the years. A recipe for every scrape, every disappointment, every heartbreak. It's his way of channeling my mother when he doesn't know what to do, what to say.

He turns and looks at us, his two girls, and only then do I see his tears.

My dad sits at the head of the table, like he always does when he's home for dinner. Mattie lowers her head, hands folded, as he recites the prayer. I fiddle with my napkin.

"Bless us, O Lord . . ."

I notice Mattie fingering my mother's gold cross necklace, which she's only once taken off, to put on a longer chain when she outgrew the old one. She mouths the words to the prayer but does not make a sound. How can she believe in a Lord that would take our mother away, would allow a girl as young as Sophie to be butchered?

". . . and these thy gifts which we are about to receive

from thy bounty, through Christ our Lord, amen."

"Amen," Mattie mutters.

I sigh loudly.

"So." My father clears his throat, reaching for a bowl of green beans. "I spoke with Sophie's parents. They're thinking the funeral will be on Tuesday." He runs his hand through his thick black hair, the way he does when he's nervous.

He tries to pass the bowl to Mattie, who makes no effort to take it from him. I reach across the table to snatch it and spoon some beans onto my plate, even though I have no appetite.

"Squeegee? Are you all right?"

Mattie is staring at nothing.

"Mattie?" My father's voice is stern. If I didn't know him so well, I'd think he was angry, not worried out of his skull. He communicates better through his kitchen creations than he does verbally.

Mattie shakes her head slightly, and her eyes focus on me, then my father.

"I'm just not very hungry. I'm going to go lie down, if that's okay?"

My father nods, and she pushes back her chair and pads softly out of the dining room.

He shifts his stare to me. I make sure my hair is hanging over the bump on my forehead so he can't see it. I don't want to explain. I don't want to talk.

After a moment, he says, "Vee, you need to eat something. You're skin and bones."

Aren't we all? Isn't that *all* we are? I saw evidence of it myself. The gory scene from the night before keeps looping through my mind. I force myself to spear some beans and stuff them into my mouth, even though I don't feel like eating.

"So how are *you* doing? Did you have any episodes this week? You've been taking your pills, haven't you?"

I make a noncommittal noise. I *have* been taking pills, but not the Provigil. Caffeine is the only thing I can count on right now—to keep me awake, to keep me from sliding back into that nightmare world. I've been popping them ever since I found Mattie on the kitchen floor.

"I'm fine," I say, choking down another forkful of green beans. "Just worry about Mattie."

He's quiet for a moment. His eyes are on his plate, his glass of water. He looks everywhere but at my face.

"You don't think she'll try anything like . . ." He can't bring himself to finish the sentence, but I know he's concerned that Mattie will do what Sophie did—well, what everyone *thinks* she did.

I've been worrying about this myself. Mattie isn't as strong as she tries to make everyone at school believe. She cried when the class hamster died—in the eighth grade. Who knows how she'll handle the death of her best friend? Right now she's in shock, but what will happen when it wears off?

I shake my head. I don't think she'd do *that*.

My father's gaze rests on Mattie's chair.

"I'm going to talk to the hospital about taking a few days off. But, Vee, if there's an emergency, I'll need you to step up and help with your sister."

I tear my eyes away from my plate and look at him. Really look at him. I long to tell him what I saw last night, how Sophie didn't really kill herself like everyone thinks she did. I want to pull him into the kitchen and force the phone into his hands and make him call the police.

But then what?

I've been down that road. I know what will happen.

No one will believe me. I'll have to start going to the shrink again. They'll probably heap some new meds on me, ones that make me into a robot, ones that make me dead inside.

No. I have to figure this out myself.

"Can I be excused?"

He studies my face, then nods. "Sure, hon."

For just a moment, I glimpse the father I used to know—the one who killed spiders and checked for monsters under my bed and made everything better with just a Band-Aid and a kiss. He looks like his old self. As I grab my plate and head for the kitchen, I try to remember the last time he looked like that. If I had to give an exact date, I would say it was before the day I tried to tell him what happens when I slide.

The day he didn't believe me.

CHAPTER SEVEN

The fluorescent light in the bathroom shines on my crime. I slide the mirror to the left, reach past an almost-full bottle of Provigil, and grab a small plastic bottle. My dad hides the Ambien way in the back of the cabinet, for when his mind is full of broken babies and he can't sleep. I mean, I get it. If it were only me standing between a six-day-old and death, the stress would get to me, too.

I shake two of the little white pills into my hand, pretty little saviors, and stick them in my pocket before filling a paper cup with water and heading toward my sister's room.

The only parts of her I can see are her fuchsia toenails. She's a lump in the bed, a mountain of blankets.

"Mattie?"

I can tell she's awake from the way the comforter wiggles. A muffled "Mmmmmph?" emerges from beneath the blanket.

"I brought you something."

She pushes down the covers and stares at me blankly.

I've never seen her this way. All our lives, she was the one who cared if her hair was brushed, if her shoes and purse matched. Now, her hair is matted in clumps. She still hasn't washed the dried mascara from her cheeks.

I sit down on the bed next to her and hold out my hand with the pills. She takes them without a word, places them in her mouth, and washes them down with the water I offer. She looks at me, and her eyes are dead.

"She won't be at school on Monday." It's as if this fact has just occurred to her.

"No."

"We were supposed to present our Spanish projects."

Mattie's face crumples, and the tears start to come. She leans toward me and buries her face in the space between my head and shoulder, making my T-shirt wet. I pat Mattie's back, feeling awkward. There's nothing to say, but I'm hoping just being here is enough.

Minutes go by, maybe even an hour.

Finally, she speaks. "It's my fault."

"No. It's not." I can't explain how I know this, but I can't let her carry around this guilt that does not belong to her. Though she's done a lot of stupid things in her life, she is not responsible for this, this thing that is bigger than both of us.

"We did something to her," she whispers, so softly I can barely hear her.

"What?" I lean closer.

"Amber and me. We did something really mean."

I remember Sophie's mother saying a true friend would never do what they did.

"What is it, Mattie?" I ask gently.

Mattie swallows a sob. "Last year Amber and I slept over at Sophie's house. We were making ice-cream sundaes, and we had a food fight. Just being dumb. Amber squirted chocolate syrup all over Sophie's hair."

"Yeah?" I prod. That doesn't sound so bad.

"While Sophie was taking a shower, Amber snuck into the bathroom and took a picture with her phone. I told her to erase it. I thought she did. Until yesterday. Amber came up with this plan to get back at Sophie for screwing around with Scotch. And I . . . I went along with it."

There's this ball of dread growing in my stomach. I don't want her to go on, but I have to hear the rest. I have to know the truth.

"What did you do?"

She takes a second to answer.

"Amber sent it to the football team."

I cover my eyes. That's what Scotch and his buddy must have been looking at on the bleachers—a picture of Sophie's naked body. Shit. I can't think of a more terrible thing to do to a girl with body issues.

"I tried to stop her. I really did. But you know Amber."

Oh, Sophie. Poor Sophie.

So that was their big plan, the one Amber was plotting in the locker room, the one intended to take Sophie down a notch. Now the scene in Sophie's bedroom—her sobbing, her mother desperately trying to comfort her—makes heartbreaking sense. But, even so, I know Sophie didn't kill herself. She was murdered.

"Do you think . . . Do you think that's why . . ." Mattie's voice breaks.

I pull Mattie closer. "That had nothing to do with her death."

"But," Mattie says, her voice no more than a ghost of a sound, "I heard there was a note. She said, 'I don't deserve this.' What else could she have been talking about?"

The memory of the letter comes rushing back. Why *did* the killer leave that note? Just to make the suicide scenario more believable? What made him—or her—choose that exact phrasing?

"I don't know," I say, trying to think of a plausible explanation to give Mattie, one that doesn't involve a psycho slaughtering her best friend. "Maybe she was just talking about her *life*."

I wish I could tell her that Sophie's death wasn't the result of a stupid prank. But, to do that, I would have to explain how I knew, and even in Mattie's state, I don't think she'd believe me.

Mattie eases back onto her pillow and yanks her pink bedspread over her head. Light from the streetlamp sneaks through the slats in her venetian blinds. I rise and pull them closed. On my way out of her room, I see the little sheep night-light she's had since she was a baby. I flip it on and leave the door open.

I wash four caffeine pills down with a swallow of Mountain Dew even though my hands are shaking and spots bounce across my field of vision. It's the only way to stay alert, to avoid the vulnerability that comes with sleepiness.

My psychology textbook is open on my bed, but I'm not able to focus on the various theories of motivation. Sophie's glassy stare keeps coming back to haunt me. Every few minutes, I relive the terror of the night before.

The terror of seeing Sophie Jacobs dead.

I hear something snap outside, and my blood runs cold. Could it be the killer? Did they realize I'd witnessed their dirty deed and come to get rid of me? I roll off my bed and crawl over to the window. I muster every ounce of courage I possess and peek out into the dark yard. There's nothing but the usual shadows twitching in the night.

Exhaling, I lower my blinds and return to my bed.

I tap my highlighter against the textbook and realize I've got to be more proactive. If I'm not going to tell the police what I saw, I have to figure out who killed Sophie Jacobs—and why. I rack my brain, reviewing every murder mystery I've ever seen on TV.

What does the hero usually do?

It seems the only place to start is to list the prime suspects. I grab my notebook and turn to a new page. Somehow, writing my thoughts down makes me feel more productive. Now. Where to start?

Well, there's Amber. Supposedly one of Sophie's best friends, she's definitely proven in the last couple of days that she has no loyalty whatsoever. And it was so weird how she fled the house this afternoon without saying a word. I jot her name down. I'm pretty sure she was jealous of Sophie—if not for her closeness with my sister, then definitely for the attention she was getting from Scotch, one of the most popular guys in school.

Ahhh, Scotch. I write down his name and underline it twice. Would-be date rapist and all-around asshole. But what motive would he have for killing Sophie?

The pieces of the puzzle are scrambled in my head, mocking me. Some of the edges are jagged, some are smooth. It seems like they should fit together, but I'm missing one piece—the most important piece.

I remember last night, how I bent down at my telescope, looking through the lens, peering at the perfect stars in the clear night sky. Something had poked me in the thigh, something sharp in my pocket.

The calendar page I'd been holding when I slid.

Holy shit.

The killer was at our house that day.

The killer . . .

Wait. That piece of paper is the biggest clue I have about who killed Sophie. I have to find it.

I toss the notebook aside and hurl myself onto the floor, searching frantically for the calendar page. There's nothing by the telescope. Maybe I accidentally kicked it under my bed in all the commotion. I lower my cheek to the carpet and peek underneath. There's nothing. Not even dust bunnies. Vanessa's so anal, she routinely pushes our beds aside and vacuums underneath.

Vanessa!

Could she have picked up the page, thinking it was garbage?

I look in my trash can. Nothing but a Target bag lining the inside.

I race downstairs. Sometimes Vanessa empties the smaller trash cans into the bigger one in the kitchen. Crossing my fingers, I pull open the cupboard below the kitchen sink and tilt the garbage can to look in. Just a banana peel. I'm about to go outside and look through the recycling bin when I smell something burning.

No. Please, no.

But I only have to step into the backyard for my hopes of using the paper to find the killer to be ruined. My father stands alone before a roaring blaze in our fire pit. He turns to look at me as I join him dejectedly.

"Seemed like a good night for a fire," he says.

CHAPTER EIGHT

In biology class on Monday, my eyes start to droop during a film about the cardiovascular system. It's been hours since my last caffeine pill. On the screen, blood cells with wide eyes and smiling little faces perform a dance and explain how they do their job. A heart bulges, filling with ruby-red fluid, then contracts, releasing the blood into the arteries.

I close my eyes and remember it all.

Her lips are parted as though she is about to say something, but she will never speak again. Black hair against white skin. The blood seeps into her bedspread, creating a red silhouette.

I wonder what her last thoughts were. I wonder whose was the last face she saw. The face I was behind. I can't catch my breath. I swallow and swallow and swallow— deep, burning mouthfuls of air, but it's not enough.

"Sylvia!" Mrs. Williams sounds far away. I feel her hands gripping me like vises, shaking me. A paper bag appears from out of nowhere, and I hold it up to my mouth to contain my panic.

Soon the fire in my chest is cooled, and I take the bag away. I look around and see dozens of eyes and gaping mouths.

"Are you okay?" Mrs. Williams asks, leaning over me.

"Yeah, I just . . . didn't sleep very well last night."

Rollins, from across the room, catches my gaze, then quickly looks away. We haven't spoken since Friday night, since I had the opportunity to open up to him but instead pushed him away. All weekend, I kept thinking he'd call me, especially after he heard about Sophie. But he never did. That'll teach me to trust someone. Right when I need them the most, they disappear. Just like my mother did. Just like my father.

Suddenly, I feel the need to get away, to be by myself.

"Would you like to get a drink of water?" I know Mrs. Williams is offering me a chance to get myself together so I don't look like such a crazy bitch. I'll take it.

"Uh, yeah."

As I rise from my desk to escape the stares, she puts her hand on my shoulder.

"We're all upset," she says quietly.

I nod and tear away from her. I feel everyone's stares as I flee from the room. Now I am not only the Narcoleptic Freak; I am the Girl Who Hyperventilated in Bio. I know they won't be talking about me at lunch today, though. Not when there's a suicide to discuss.

In the hallway, I look up one way and down the other. No one. The bathroom is only across the hall, but the walk drains me. I make sure the room is empty and lock myself in the stall farthest from the door. The same one

Sophie was in on Friday morning.

My head throbs. Kneading my temples with my fingers, I stare at the graffiti on the stall door. *RIP Sophie.* I reach out and touch the words, the cool metal. On Friday, Sophie was here in the flesh, and now she is only words carved into red paint.

Rest in peace. The sentiment is nice, but when it's shortened like that—RIP—it reminds me of Sophie's ivory skin, ripped open like tissue paper. I turn around and retch into the toilet.

Minutes later, as I rinse my face off in the sink, the intercom crackles. Miss Lamb, the secretary, tearfully announces that Sophie Jacobs will be greatly missed. She says school tomorrow will be let out early for Sophie's funeral. If any of us need to talk to someone about our loss, the counselor has cleared her schedule. This makes me laugh bitterly. If I wanted to explain my predicament to the counselor, she'd have to clear her schedule for a year.

At lunchtime, I avoid the bleachers. I don't want to talk to Rollins, and the memory of Scotch and his buddy peering at the picture of Sophie sickens me. I wander the halls aimlessly.

I pass by Mr. Golden's room and see him eating a slice of pizza at his desk. His room seems homey and warm compared to the rest of the school. I find myself lingering in his doorway, wanting to just curl up on one of his couches and go to sleep.

"Sylvia? Are you all right?"

I'm shaken by his voice. He's holding his slice of pizza inches away from his mouth, like he was just about to take a bite when he was interrupted by some emo girl in the hallway.

"Oh, I'm sorry. I'll just . . ." I gesture at a random point down the hall and start to leave.

"No, wait." He puts the pizza down, stands, and takes several steps in my direction. "Come in. Please."

I try not to sigh audibly as I take shelter in his room and fall onto one of his couches. So. Tired. My fingers move to my pocket, to the Provigil bottle full of my sacred caffeine, but then I realize Mr. Golden might report me if he sees me munching on a bunch of pills. I decide to wait, just a little longer.

Mr. Golden closes the door and sinks into a nearby recliner. We sit in silence for a few moments. This is what I need right now. Time to think. Space to exist. The tension melts from my shoulders as I become one with the smelly old couch, just another odd relic in Mr. Golden's collection of weird things.

"Do you ever feel like life is too messed up for words?" I finally ask Mr. Golden. The strangeness of the past few days makes them seem unreal, like it was all just a movie. One I can't escape.

"All the time," he says, nodding.

I stare at my chipped black nail polish. "I just don't get how one person can completely destroy another person."

I'm thinking of the way the knife curved in the killer's hands, covered in Sophie's blood, how it seemed like Sophie wasn't even a person anymore—she was just another inanimate object in the room, robbed of her humanness.

"Are we talking about Sophie?" Mr. Golden's question is soft and cautious. He asks it in a way that is the opposite of how the school counselor might ask it. His voice isn't clinical. There are no ulterior motives. He just sounds curious.

"Yeah." I release a deep breath. I can feel the pressure of it all growing within me, a dam about to burst. Maybe there is a way I can talk around what happened, sort of. Not go into details or anything, but just take the edge off a little bit. "She was friends with my sister."

He leans forward. "That must be hard. How is Mattie doing?"

I pick at my nails. "Not so good. She feels like . . . like she might have had something to do with Sophie's death. She did something not very nice to Sophie the day she died."

"That's rough." Mr. Golden rubs at his beard thoughtfully. "But no one made Sophie kill herself. It's important to realize that. Her choice was her own. It's a terrible thing, but no one put that knife in Sophie's hand."

I drop my hands into my lap abruptly.

How did he know about the knife? Did the teachers hear all the gory details during a faculty meeting?

He winces a little and pulls back. "I realize that must sound harsh to you, Vee. But suicide really is an act of selfishness. Think of her parents. Think of her friends, who are left to wonder what they could have done to stop it.

Whatever your sister did, it wasn't enough to drive Sophie to take her own life."

"But Sophie didn't—" Somehow, I stop myself from insisting that Sophie didn't kill herself. How could I explain without telling my secret?

"Sophie didn't what, Vee?" Mr. Golden tenses, his fingers curling against his khakis.

I drum my fingers against my leg in frustration. How can I make him understand?

"I just feel like Sophie would never do something like that." I remember Sophie's mother's words. "She was strong—more than she knew."

Mr. Golden's face softens. "That's very nice of you to say, Vee. But you can't know how she was feeling. Depression is an insidious monster. It eats you up from the inside. No, I think Sophie was in an immense amount of pain."

I dig my fingers into my temples and rub little circles. Nothing I say, short of confessing I witnessed the murder, will change Mr. Golden's mind. In just a few seconds, Mr. Golden has morphed into an authority figure, spouting off crap about things he can't possibly know. I really thought he was different.

I stand indignantly.

"There's more to Sophie's death. And I'm going to find out what it is."

I turn to leave before he can say anything in response, but the look on his face is so satisfying—his eyebrows raised and jaw dropped. I hope someday the truth does come out, and he remembers all this psychobabble bullshit he tried to feed me.

When I open the door, I come face-to-face with Samantha Phillips, who's gazing into a mirror on her locker door and patting powder onto her prissy little nose. She looks from me to the dimly lit room from which I've just emerged. Her eyes light up with glee, probably thinking about the rumors she can spread. By the end of the day, everyone will be whispering about my scandalous affair with Mr. Golden.

"Doing a little extra credit?" she asks, smirking.

I scowl at her and walk away. The sound of her voice reminds me of locker rooms and purple dresses and hands where they shouldn't be.

"Better be careful," she calls after me. "Sophie Jacobs got cozy with Mr. G., and look where she is now."

I stop abruptly and turn to confront her. "What are you talking about?"

She closes her locker door. "I saw her with him. In his car. All I'm saying is, you better be careful. He likes 'em young." She spins on her heel and heads in the other direction, snickering all the way.

And then it hits me. *I* saw them together, too. It was Sophie shaking and crying on the couch in Mr. Golden's room. Hours before she was murdered.

CHAPTER NINE

I arrive late to psychology, but Mr. Golden doesn't give me a tardy. In fact, he doesn't say anything to me at all, doesn't even look at me, just keeps talking about intrinsic versus extrinsic motivation.

Scanning the room, I realize there are only two places left to sit—next to Rollins or next to Zane. Just as he did in biology, Rollins looks at me and then away.

I drop my eyes and sink into the empty seat next to Zane, pulling out my notebook. Mr. Golden roams around as he talks, alternately poking his finger in the air and tugging at his beard. His voice is higher than normal, and he seems like he's had about twenty cups of coffee because his sentences don't really make sense. They're just a jumble of words.

What exactly happened in here on Friday?

Why would Sophie be crying to Mr. Golden?

He's a good teacher, and I can see someone feeling like they could confide in him. Maybe Sophie came in here after she found out Amber sent that naked picture of her to everyone. Or maybe she was having problems with Scotch and went to Mr. Golden seeking advice.

Or *maybe* Samantha is right for once in her life.

Maybe Sophie and Mr. Golden *were* having an affair.

He's good-looking in an older, Johnny Depp sort of way. I could see how a girl could develop a crush on him. And what guy wouldn't want some of what Sophie had? She was stunning.

But she was a kid.

My stomach turns over, thinking about the two of them together.

"You okay?" A hand pulls on my sleeve, bringing me back from my twisted reverie. Zane is leaning close, and I catch a whiff of his cologne, something spicy.

He's got a notebook propped up on his lap so that it looks like he's taking notes, but behind it he's reading a book. I crane my head to see the title—*Tender Is the Night*. Zane catches me peeking and gives me a sheepish, lopsided grin.

I smile back, and warmth rushes into my cheeks. It's nice to feel something other than fear. It's nice to think about how cute Zane is, with that shock of blond hair falling in his face, instead of speculating about who killed Sophie. Zane returns to his book, and I try to focus on what Mr. Golden is saying. I realize someone is staring at me from across the room. It's Rollins, and he doesn't look happy at all.

———

After class, Rollins pushes out of the room without a word, but Zane lingers as I stuff my notebook into my backpack.

"Good weekend?"

"Um. Not exactly."

He gives me a sideways look. "Everything okay?"

"Well, besides my sister's best friend dying, I'm great," I say, and then realize how bitter that sounds. "Sorry. Just having a rough week."

He reaches toward me, as if to put a hand on my arm, but then pulls it away, like he's not sure if he should touch me. "I'm sorry to hear that."

Determined not to be a total downer, I try to make small talk. "So how was your weekend?"

He shrugs. "Went to a concert."

"Oh, yeah? Who'd you see?"

"The Belly-Button Lint."

"Never heard of 'em."

"Consider yourself lucky." He makes a face and tucks his novel under his arm.

"Good book?" I ask.

Zane grins. "I'm a sucker for Fitzgerald."

"Yeah? I read *The Great Gatsby* last year. Not a huge fan."

We're the last ones in the classroom, and I'm conscious of Mr. Golden straightening papers at his desk, trying to seem like he's not listening.

"Let me guess. You read it for English. You had to fill out study guides. At the end, you wrote a five-page paper and had to analyze the characters, the symbols, the theme." Zane shakes his head in disgust.

"Something like that," I say, nodding. It was only a three-page paper, but still.

"God, it pisses me off when teachers suck all the life out of literature. Do me a favor. Read *Gatsby* again, but read it outside, under a tree, at dusk. It's a completely different experience. Only read a chapter if you want, but give it a shot. Will you do that for me?"

The expression on his face is so serious. I've never met anyone as passionate about words before. Well, Rollins loves to write, but it's almost as though he does it because he's compelled to point out the hypocrisy all around us, not because he loves the language. The way Zane speaks about F. Scott Fitzgerald—well, it reminds me of how I feel about the stars. They are bigger than me, bigger than us all, and that's what makes them beautiful.

"I promise," I say, and the look on Zane's face makes me tingle.

After school, a handful of kids are hanging out in the parking lot, killing time before football practice or play rehearsal or whatever. A group of guys sits in the back of a pickup truck, arguing about who will buy beer next weekend. Two sophomore girls lean together, sharing earbuds, bopping their heads to a beat I can't hear.

I pass by the tree Sophie, Mattie, and Amber used to hang out under. I can picture her easy smile and dimples. *Her wide-open eyes. The dark slash across each wrist. The white piece of paper, mocking me with Sophie's fake last words.* I have to stop walking. I drop my backpack and lean against the tree, pressing my palms into my eyelids to make the memory go away.

When I remove my hands, I see the girls have stopped dancing. They stare at me from a distance, probably trying to avoid catching the crazy from me. I straighten up, try to look normal, or as normal as a pink-haired narcoleptic can appear.

A hand reaches out and grabs me.

"Aaaaaaaaaaaaaaiiiiiiiiii!"

Rollins emerges from behind the tree, a cigarette dangling from his mouth. His leather jacket hangs open, revealing a Decemberists T-shirt.

"Hey, it's just me."

I catch my breath, glaring at him. How can he ignore me all weekend, especially after Sophie's death, and then expect me to act like nothing's wrong?

"Why were you hiding behind a tree?" I demand. "Are you trying to give me a heart attack?"

The two girls are still gaping at me, and Rollins takes a few steps toward them and thrusts out his hands, curved like claws. "Boo!" They move away nervously.

When he returns, he gives me an apologetic look. "I'm sorry. I didn't mean to scare you. Nasty said he'd give me a month of detention if he caught me smoking again, so I was kinda lying low."

I wait for a moment, expecting him to apologize for barging out so suddenly on Friday night or at least to make some comment about Sophie's death. But instead he just looks at his shoes, his hands pushed deep in his pockets.

"So what happened in bio today? I was going to ask you in psychology, but you seemed busy," he says, practically spitting the last word.

If he hadn't been so absent lately, I might tell him the truth, how I can't quite shake the feeling that the world is a few shades darker since Sophie died. How I'm scared of my own shadow. If he'd really wanted to know, he would have called me. He would have come after me when I freaked out in bio. He would have stuck around to talk to me after psychology, not gotten pissed that I was having a conversation with someone who actually seems to care how I feel.

The lie, not quite a lie but not quite the truth, comes out easily—the same one I told Mrs. Williams. "It was nothing. I just haven't been sleeping well. A lot of stress, you know?"

He squints at me, and I feel like he's staring right through the brave front I've been putting up all day. "Right. Well, how is Mattie?"

"How would you feel if your best friend died?" I give him a stink eye that would rival Mrs. Winger's, hoping to make him realize just how stupid his question is.

He holds my gaze steadily. "Pretty shitty, I guess."

"Yeah. She's feeling pretty shitty."

We stand there, looking at each other. His face is blank.

"Why didn't you call?" I demand finally. "I mean, you must have heard what happened on Friday night."

His eyes drop away from my face. I can see I've caught him off guard. It's obvious we're growing apart, but it's like he didn't expect me to say anything about it. I guess I

don't blame him, really. I'm not usually big on confronta-
tion.

"I don't know," he says, shuffling his feet. "I was busy
at home. Besides, if you needed to talk, you could have
called me."

He meets my eyes again, and this time I have to look
away. It's true. I could have called him. But I didn't. If
only I could reach out to him, ask for help, tell him what's
going on with me. Every time I picture it, though, I see my
father's face when I told him about sliding—how panicked
he was, how he clearly thought I was crazy.

I can't go through that again.

After a long silence, he picks my backpack up off the
ground from where I dropped it. He hands it to me.

"Heavy."

"Yeah," I mutter, swinging the bag over my shoulder.
"It's really heavy."

I want him to say something else, something light
and funny to make everything between us better. But he
doesn't say anything, just stands there. I wish I knew how
to get back to *us* again, but something's broken between us,
and no matter how much I want to—I can't fix it.

CHAPTER TEN

The leaves crunch beneath my feet as I make my way home. Only a few stragglers remain on the branches, and some of those drop to the ground when the wind picks up. A yellow leaf twirls and dances to the ground before me.

Strange how death can be so beautiful.

I immediately feel guilty for the thought. Sophie did not look beautiful. She looked drained and defeated, like life had beaten her. I try to think of something else, but she's always in the back of my mind, waiting for me. Somewhere, right now, her killer is carrying on with life, believing he (or she) got away with it.

I pull my jacket tighter, but the wind cuts right through the thin fabric. Long shadows grow from the trees and the mailboxes. On a lawn grown over with weeds, an abandoned tricycle is tipped on its side. It looks so old and rusty, I bet the child who used to ride it around is halfway through college by now.

I'm a few houses down from ours, taking in our buttery-yellow Victorian with green shutters. My father hires a neighborhood boy to come rake the leaves and put them in fat plastic bags on the curb. You can tell he hasn't come in a while because the leaves have covered most of the lawn, obscuring the dying grass.

Our house looks so normal from the outside. If you were a stranger passing by, you might think a perfectly nice, average family lived inside—one with a mother and a loving father and two well-adjusted teenage girls. You'd never know the mother was long gone or that the father lived in an impenetrable shell or that one of the girls could slide into you and see the things you hide from everyone.

Suddenly, I feel sure that someone's watching me. I spin around, but no one's there. It's the same sleepy neighborhood I've known all my life. Empty street. People tucked away in their houses, probably watching TV or playing on the internet or cooking dinner. Still the feeling remains. Shuddering, I pull my sweatshirt tight around me and climb the front porch.

My father is in his study, bent over his laptop. He's got white earbuds in, but a few stray notes escape and I recognize Mozart. My father looks like the exact opposite of my mother. While her hair was long and blond, his is dark and frizzy. She was curvy, with full cheeks; he is lean to the point of looking gaunt. Usually he's clean-shaven, but today he's got stubble.

His fingers fly over the keyboard in a productive little dance. He *tap-tap-tap*s, then stops to take a sip from a glass of ice water, then taps some more.

"Hey, Dad?"

He's totally absorbed in his own little world and just keeps on tapping. I pluck a bud from his ears and say louder, "Dad!"

A shadow of annoyance crosses his face, but it's gone in an instant. I know he doesn't like to be disturbed when he's on the computer, which he is practically every second he's not at the hospital or concocting some masterpiece in the kitchen.

He moderates an online forum for people who've lost loved ones to cancer. There's something ironic about it, how he spends all his free time healing strangers on the internet while Mattie and I are holed up in our rooms by ourselves.

"Hey, Dad. Where's Mattie?"

"In her room, sleeping. I was wondering if you'd go with her to the funeral tomorrow?"

I shift my bag from one arm to the other. Suddenly, the weight is unbearable.

"You're not going?"

He squirms. "I made a quiche for the family. Took it over today while you were at school. I've got to work tomorrow."

My stomach starts to ache. I really don't want to see Sophie again, but someone has to go with Mattie. Someone has to be the adult.

"I guess I'll go. I'm tired. Going to lie down for a while. See you at dinner."

He brightens. "I'm making a pot roast."

The thought of a big hunk of meat makes me *muy verde*—as Señora Gomez would say—but I try to be polite. "Yum."

I wander into the family room and drop my bag on the floor. From the mantel, I grab my parents' wedding photo. My father looks strong and happy, and my mother is positively glowing. Staring at the picture, I flop down onto the couch. If only my mother were here, she'd know what to do. She'd go to Sophie's funeral and hold Mattie's hand and do all the motherly stuff.

I must be sleepier than I thought, because I fall asleep, clutching the picture to my chest.

I'm running through the woods behind our house, branches scraping at my face and bare arms. She's here, somewhere. Who I'm looking for, I'm not quite sure, but the need to find her surges through my veins like fire.

I have to save her.

Something inside me says to run toward the stream. I can see it up ahead, the water glistening in a few places where the sun shines through.

As I get closer, I can see something in the water, among the logs and pebbles. The water is shallow here, and I glimpse a red-and-gold skirt that looks unnatural against the greens and browns. Pale skin underwater. Long strands of black hair waving around a swollen face.

It is Sophie.

Blood wisps from her wrists in long, skinny strands.

I sink to my knees at the water's edge and moan up at the

unforgiving trees. I'm too late. She is gone forever. I cover my eyes and start to cry.

"Why are you crying?" someone asks, and I uncover my face.

The body is sitting up!

Scrambling backward, I slip on a root and end up flat on my back. Sophie reaches for me with fingers like claws.

I open my mouth to scream, but my voice is gone.

The Sophie thing grabs my shoulders and leans closer. I can smell her breath, the decay of it, like something sweet gone rotten.

"What's wrong, Vee? Feeling guilty?"

Her grasp tightens, and I feel like her fingernails are going to break my skin. Her eyes are black, soulless, nothing like the sweet girl I knew.

"Are you feeling bad you didn't do anything when you had the chance?"

Inside her mouth are tiny, pointed teeth. Sharp enough to tear flesh.

"You let them hurt me, Vee. You didn't say anything. Did you?"

I start to cry, tears stinging my cheeks. "I'm sorry, Sophie. I wanted to help you. I did. I just didn't know how—"

"Bullshit," she hisses. "You. Let. Me. Die."

Her mouth drops open like she has no jaw, and all I can see are those sharp little teeth that are going to chew me to bits. And I know I deserve it.

CHAPTER ELEVEN

A noise tears me from my nightmare. I sit straight up, heart pounding, sure that Sophie's come to our house to get me.

Bing bong. Bing bong. Bing bong.

No. It's just the doorbell.

Sophie's not here. Sophie is dead.

The late afternoon light slants through the dusty air of our family room and hits the scuffed wood floor. I pull myself up and stagger toward the door, passing my dad's study on the way. His head sways to a beat I can't hear—too loud, obviously, for him to hear the doorbell.

A tall man with serious eyes stands on our front porch. He's dressed in a police uniform. Shit. How could the cops know I was there when Sophie died? I force my face to relax.

"Hello. I'm Officer Teahen. Are you Mattie Bell?"

"Uh, no. That's my sister. Has she done something wrong?"

He releases a puff of air and says, "Oh, no, no. I just

need to ask her some questions. She was friends with Sophie Jacobs, correct?"

Before I can answer, I feel a warm hand on my shoulder. "Can I help you?" My father inches in front of me a bit, blocking the open door.

"Mr. Bell," the officer says politely. "I was wondering if I could speak with your daughter Mattie about Sophie Jacobs. I'd like to get an idea of the frame of mind she was in on Friday before . . . before the incident. Is she available?"

The muscles in my father's hand tense, but he gives a perfectly cordial reply. "She's up in her room. Let me see if she's awake." He steps back, pulling me with him, and opens the door wide for the policeman to step through.

"Would you like something to drink, Officer . . . ?"

"Teahen. Officer Teahen," the man replies, stepping into our front entryway. "Some water would be great."

My father pats me on the back with a little pressure in the direction of the kitchen, and I continue on my trajectory to fetch a glass of water. Too curious to even be annoyed with the task, I grab a Scooby-Doo glass out of the cupboard and wait for the water to run cold before filling it.

When I return, Mattie is sitting in the recliner, and my father and the officer are stationed on the couch. I hand the glass of water to the policeman, and he takes a long gulp before setting it on the coffee table. I slink backward and take a seat on the bottom step, where no one can see me, but I can hear everything.

Officer Teahen clears his throat. "Well, Mattie, can you start by telling me a little about your friendship with Sophie?"

A pause hangs in the air, and I know exactly what Mattie is thinking about. The naked pictures Amber sent to the football team—does the officer know? Is that something *friends* do?

When she speaks, I can hear the nervousness in her voice. "We've been best friends since the eighth grade. We were in cheerleading together. I—I loved her." Mattie's words dissolve into a string of hiccups and sobs.

Everyone is quiet for a little bit, until Mattie stops crying.

The officer speaks again, a bit more warmly. "I'm very sorry for your loss, Mattie. Don't be nervous. I just want to know how she was feeling that day. Did she seem a little off to you? When was the last time you spoke with her?"

Mattie starts to sound a little more confident. "Friday morning, at her locker. She said she wasn't feeling very well. She thought the cinnamon roll she got in the cafeteria must have been bad."

"I see. Did she seem depressed at all to you?"

"No, just sick." I think of Sophie puking up her breakfast in the bathroom stall, right before I slid into Amber and witnessed her plotting to take Sophie down a notch.

"Okay," Officer Teahen says. "So you didn't see her at all on Friday night?"

"No. I went to cheerleading practice with Amber. Sophie wasn't there, but I figured she was just sick or something. Samantha gave us a ride home, and Amber spent the night."

"Did you and Amber stay here all night?"

There's a long pause. She's probably calculating which will get her into more trouble—lying to a cop or facing my father's fury.

"No," Mattie says finally, sounding guilty. "We went to a party."

I slap my hand against the wooden stairs and then wince, hoping they didn't hear me. This is news to me. She said she and Amber were going to the movies with Samantha. What a little liar.

"The one on College Street?"

My sister is quiet.

"I talked to Amber already," the officer explains. "I just want to corroborate that you did indeed attend the frat party. You won't get in trouble, at least not with me. Just answer truthfully."

My father cuts in. "Listen, should I have my lawyer here for this?"

"No, no. Like I said, I just want to make sure I have a good idea about what happened that night. Mattie, it's okay to tell me what happened. You went to the party? And then what?"

My sister speaks slowly. "And then we went to Marty's for breakfast."

Marty's is an all-night diner that caters to the college crowd. There are always drunk kids in the wee hours of the morning, demanding coffee or pie or, in my sister's case, a ginormous plate of pancakes. Rollins and I sometimes go there after a particularly long movie marathon.

"And what time was this?"

"Around eleven."

"What time did you get home from Marty's?"

"Maybe two?"

"Was Amber with you?"

"No. Samantha and I went to breakfast. Amber disappeared. I didn't see her again until the morning, when she crawled into my bed, all hungover."

"How did she get back into the house if she didn't come home with you?"

"I left the door unlocked."

Silence. I assume the officer is jotting something on his notepad.

I rest my head on my knees, doing the math. Amber was unaccounted for between eleven on Friday night and when I saw her the next morning. Plenty of time to—to what? Sneak over to Sophie's house? Slit her wrists? Arrange a suicide note? That's ridiculous. Isn't it? Amber may have been jealous of Sophie, but does that make her a killer?

"So you didn't speak to Sophie at all on Friday night?"

"No, sir," my sister sniffles.

"Then why did Sophie's parents receive a call from this residence around midnight demanding they look in on her?"

Oh God. I hadn't thought of the cops tracing that call. This isn't good.

Mattie is sputtering. "I—I don't know what you're talking about."

I stand. "Officer Teahen, that was me."

He looks at me in surprise, as if he'd forgotten all about the pink-haired girl who answered the door. I step into the living room. Time to think of a good lie. Fast.

"Mattie wasn't home yet," I explain. "I wasn't sure where she was. I was looking for her. I thought she might be at

Sophie's house. That's why I asked her parents to check."

My father's face relaxes, but the officer continues to eye me. Finally, he makes a note and returns his gaze to my sister.

"Okay. One more question, Mattie. Were you aware that Sophie was pregnant?"

I gasp and look at Mattie. Her mouth is open as she stares at the officer in astonishment. It's pretty clear Mattie didn't know anything about a pregnancy.

"I see." The officer nods and stands. "Thank you very much. I 'preciate it." He shakes my father's hand and then heads to the door.

My dad waits a good thirty seconds before he starts yelling. "A party? On fraternity row? What were you thinking? I can't believe you, Mattie. What do you have to say for yourself?"

My sister's face crumbles under my father's scrutiny. "I'm sorry," she cries. "I'm sorry. I'm sorry. I'm sorry. I'm sorry."

She covers her face and runs up the stairs, pushing me out of the way. My father sighs and follows her, showing with his posture that he'd rather be doing anything but calming a hysterical teenage girl.

I float over to the couch, shocked. Sophie was *pregnant?* On Friday morning, when she was puking in the bathroom—that must have been morning sickness. And Scotch mentioned on the bleachers that he'd slept with her. He must have gotten her pregnant.

Maybe Scotch isn't the father, though. What if Samantha is right, and Sophie was sleeping with Mr. Golden? If he was the father, he'd have a lot to lose—his job, for starters.

Would his teaching position be so important to him that he'd kill to keep it?

My phone buzzes to life in my pocket, interrupting my thoughts. I answer the phone absentmindedly.

"Hey, Vee. What's up?" Rollins's voice sounds strained.

"Listen, I'm kind of busy. What do you need?" I wince as soon as the words are out of my mouth. They sound terrible.

"Look. I'm trying to make an effort."

I take a deep breath. "I know. I'm sorry. Things are just really stressful. An officer was here, questioning my sister."

"Really?"

"Yeah. It was messed up."

We're both quiet for a second.

"Hey, I'm sorry I haven't been around much lately," he says. "I'm kind of going through some intense stuff of my own."

I think of how he's never let me visit his house. What's going on over there?

"You want to talk about it?"

"No. It's personal." His voice sounds strangled, like he wants to tell me what's going on with him but can't bring himself to spill his guts. I know how that feels. I wish, more than anything, that he felt comfortable sharing his problems, but how can I pressure him when I have my own secrets?

"Well. If you ever want to talk, you know I'm here."

"I know," he says. "Hey. We cool?"

"We cool," I reply. "Wanna go to a funeral with me tomorrow?"

CHAPTER TWELVE

Mattie rides silently in the back of Rollins's car. We circle the parking lot, looking for an available space, but there's nothing. Even the handicapped spots are all full. We have to park on the street a block down from the funeral home and walk the rest of the way.

Wind sweeps through my hair and chills my skin. Normally I wouldn't think twice about huddling next to Rollins for warmth, but our relationship seems fragile now, like a bone that's broken and not yet fully healed. It seems safer to keep to myself.

We are a parade of black. Rollins wears jeans, a black button-down shirt, and a skinny black tie. I picked out a pair of simple black pants and a nice black shirt edged with dark-purple lace. My sister is wearing the slinky black dress she'd planned on wearing to homecoming. I didn't have the heart to point out how inappropriate it was. She doesn't really own any other black clothes.

Despite the chill in the air outside, it feels like an oven when we push into the building. The place is packed wall to wall with people, who drift from one homemade Sophie photo collage to another, as if they're in a museum.

In one picture, Sophie looks about age six, chubby in a blue tutu and mouse nose and whiskers and ears. In another, she hooks her arms around Mattie's and Amber's shoulders, all of them in their cheerleading uniforms. Time spins backward in another picture, and baby Sophie plays in a duck-shaped bathtub, a washcloth modestly placed over her girly parts.

Sophie's mother bustles over, her teased hair leading the way, and gives Mattie a hug. Tears squeeze out of her eyes, blue makeup running in streams through the creases in her face. She looks haggard.

"I'm so glad you could make it," she says, and Mattie reaches her arms around Mrs. Jacobs for a hug.

"I'm sorry," Mattie whispers. The words are not enough, can never be enough, and it's like we're all standing around the growing hole of how *not enough* they are. Sophie's mom squeezes Mattie once more and leaves to make her rounds.

We trudge toward the next room, where row upon row of folding chairs have been set up. Most of them are already taken by Sophie's extended family and teachers and what seems like every kid in the whole school. We're lucky to find three seats in the back.

I sit between Mattie and Rollins and crane my head, searching every face, but I don't see anyone I'm looking for. No Amber. No Scotch. No Mr. Golden.

It takes about fifteen minutes for everyone to get settled. Tons of people have to stand in the back of the sweltering room. They fan themselves with programs that have Sophie's school picture on the cover.

The coffin is at the front, flanked by long white candles and great bouquets of lilies. Thank God it's a closed casket. I don't know if I could handle seeing her again. My sister sobs quietly next to me. I take her hand.

A slim man in a blue suit finds his way to the front and stands before the casket, his hands hovering just above the white wood but not touching it. He stands there reverently for a moment, and everyone tries not to stare. Someone behind me whispers that he's Sophie's father. He turns around to face us, his lower lip wobbling, but he composes himself long enough to read a poem he has written for Sophie.

Almost everyone's head is down, giving the man his time to mourn, but I'm looking around the room, hoping to spot one of my suspects, to see how they're reacting to all this.

After the man has finished his poem, an old woman plays a piano in the corner. I mutter something about having to go to the bathroom and manage to edge my way out of our row and through the crowd without sticking my butt in anyone's face or knocking anyone over.

I duck out a door in the back that leads to a smaller room with a blue couch and an end table loaded with boxes of Kleenex. There's a pop machine and a water cooler in the corner. Doors on either side of the room lead to the bathrooms. I hear a strange sound coming from the ladies' room—almost like honking.

I twist the knob and push open the door just a crack, enough to peek inside and see who's making the terrible noise. Crumpled on the floor with a wad of toilet paper woven around her fingers, Amber Prescott is falling apart.

I slip into the room and close the door behind me. Then I sink to the floor and sit across from Amber, cross-legged. I don't say anything, don't even look at her. I just sit and breathe. And wait.

Amber stops crying long enough to recognize who's in the room with her, but then she continues on, louder than ever. In her place, I would have shouted to get the hell out. I don't do anything but let her raw emotion wash over me. Though it seems like she's truly devastated, I can't help but wonder how much of what I'm seeing is guilt. Guilt for destroying her best friend.

Just when I start to think about going to get her a cup of water, she stops crying. She uses the toilet paper to clean up the mascara that's run all over her face. I stand up and turn on the water for her, then step out of the way so she can wash her face.

She doesn't say anything to me, just gives me this kind of grateful look before she opens the door and slinks out. When she leaves, I glance in the mirror, at the girl with the pink pigtails tied with black ribbons, and all I feel is shame. Amber may have ruined Sophie, but I stood by and let her. I knew Amber and Mattie were planning something horrible, and I didn't do one damn thing to stop them.

As I open the door to leave, I notice something silver shining on the floor. I look closer and realize it's a tiny diamond earring—the kind that Amber always wears. I scoop it up and hurry out of the bathroom to see if I can catch her, but I don't see her anywhere. I tuck the earring into my pocket.

The funeral has ended, and people have formed small clusters around the lobby.

I spot Mattie in a huddle of cheerleaders doing some sort of group hug, but I don't see Rollins anywhere so I go outside. Just as I'd guessed, Rollins is standing several yards away from the funeral home, a cigarette tucked discreetly behind his back.

"Everyone's saying Sophie was pregnant," Rollins says, taking a quick drag and then hiding the cigarette again.

I sigh. "Yeah. The officer mentioned something about it yesterday."

"You have any idea who the father could be?" Rollins releases a puff of smoke.

"I have a few theories," I reply. "The front-runner is Scotch Becker."

Rollins drops the cigarette and grinds it into the cement with the heel of his boot. "Scum."

"Pretty much."

A hand on my back makes me jump. Turning, I see Mattie's teary face.

"You ready to go?" I ask. Earlier, Mattie had cried that she didn't want to go to the burial. She didn't want to see Sophie's casket lowered into the ground. I can't say I blame her.

"Actually," she says, "I think I'm going to stay. Sam can

give me a ride." She glances behind her, and I follow her gaze to Samantha Phillips, who stands twirling her keys. When she sees me looking, her face goes slack and she turns to face the other way.

"Are you sure?" I ask.

She nods.

"Okay, I'll see you at home."

I watch her return to the group of cheerleaders. It seems strange—of all the people saying good-bye to Sophie today, I'm the only one who knows how she truly left this world. The knowledge settles at the bottom of my stomach and weighs me down like cement.

Rollins squeezes my shoulder. "Let's go."

CHAPTER THIRTEEN

Long after Rollins drops me off, I sit on the swing on our front porch. I don't want to go inside. The house is so empty. So silent. I don't want to be alone with my memory of Sophie's death. I don't want to risk falling asleep and having to face her accusations again. Outside, the wind keeps me awake. That, and the caffeine pills.

I shake some more into my hand, pop them into my mouth, and crunch them into powder.

A breeze blows through the large oak tree, coaxing even more leaves to fall. Down the street, a movement catches my eye. A tall boy with a cobalt sweatshirt and blond hair is making his way toward me on a skateboard. As he gets closer, I see that it's Zane Huxley. And he's looking in my direction. My stomach does a little somersault.

He coasts to a stop in front of my house, flips up his skateboard, and takes a few steps toward the porch. "Hey," he says, an unmistakable look of pleasure crossing his face.

I nod at him, swallowing the caffeine powder so I can speak. "Hey. Enjoying your afternoon off from school?"

"Yeah. Did you go to the funeral?"

"Yeah. It was . . . unfathomable," I say, unable to find a more fitting word for the funeral of a teenager. "What are you doing here, anyway?"

I feel dumb and want to take back the question. It sounds like I don't want him here, when I do. I want someone to talk to. Someone who didn't know Sophie, someone who doesn't know about me and my narcolepsy and how messed up everything is.

Luckily, he just laughs. "Good to see you, too. We live over on Arbor Lane, at the end of the street."

"The blue one with the picket fence? That's been for sale forever."

An awkward silence passes between us. I try to think of something funny or clever or *anything* to say. I don't want to be alone with my thoughts anymore.

Another gust of wind rips through the yard, sending a chill through me. I shiver.

"Hey, do you want to come in? I could make some coffee or something."

"Sure. Little chilly outside."

I get up and open the door, and he props up his skateboard outside and follows me into the house. In the kitchen, he pulls out a stool and sits with his elbows on the counter. I whisk two coffee mugs—one from the University of Iowa and one that says "Bestest Dad in the World"—out of the cupboard and set them between us. He's quiet as I make the coffee, and it reminds me of sitting in the bathroom of the funeral home, giving Amber the time to put herself back together.

I fill each mug with steaming black liquid. In the refrigerator, I find half a gallon of skim milk. I dump some in my cup and then spoon in a little sugar. After stirring it for a few seconds, I take a sip.

Over the rim of my cup, I watch Zane stirring milk into his coffee with his finger. I can't believe he's here, in my kitchen. It's almost enough to make me forget about the murder, about the way Sophie's mouth was slightly open, a trickle of blood escaping it. Almost.

Zane winks at me. "You look cute in pigtails."

"Thanks," I say, braving a smile.

His eyes are so deep and blue, I could get lost in them.

An hour later, I'm sprawled on the couch, clutching my coffee, and Zane is lazily sipping his own drink only inches away. I can see his knee through a large rip in his jeans. The hair on his legs is fine and blond, just like the hair on his head. I fight the urge to reach over and stroke it.

"So you used to live in Iowa City?" I try to make my voice sound sexy and throaty, but it actually comes out kind of squeaky.

"Yeah. I was born here. Moved to Chicago when I was little. Mom wanted to come back. No offense, but I'm not a big fan of Iowa." He smiles apologetically. His teeth are so white. Light blond stubble covers his square jaw. I want to feel it against my cheek, my lips. My proximity to him seems to have narrowed my focus, and all I can see is his face.

"Not many people are," I reply.

Zane picks up a picture of me, my sister, and my dad.

"What does your dad do?" He gestures to the photo.

"He's a pediatric surgeon," I say. "Today he's operating on some kid who was born with his bowels on the outside."

Zane shakes his head. "That's pretty impressive. I mean, your dad's job, not the baby with the guts on the outside."

"I know," I say, a hint of bitterness in my words.

"How about your mom?" We both look down at the picture in his hands, at the space where a mother should be, but isn't.

I'm a little surprised he'd be so bold as to ask such a question when it's clear my mom is either dead or off somewhere else, leading a life that doesn't include me, but I remember him on his first day, telling me that his father was dead. It feels like a natural course for our conversation.

"Pancreatic cancer. She died when I was eleven."

He nods, as though I've confirmed what he'd suspected. "That's gotta be rough on a kid."

I peer into my coffee cup. "It was. I mean, it still is. It doesn't help that my dad is gone all the time. I've pretty much become my sister's parent. He didn't even come home to help take care of her when we found out about Sophie's death."

He makes a sympathetic noise. "I know what you mean. My mom hasn't really been herself in years. Ever since my father died, she's been living in her own little world."

"So how old were you when your father died?"

"He killed himself when I was three." The matter-of-fact way he says it shocks me into silence.

"It's cool," Zane says, as if to reassure me that there's no right response to that news. "I don't really remember him. I was too young. I've got this picture of us, though—of him and me. He was pushing me on the swing. And he's smiling really big with his mouth, but you can see in his eyes—he's not happy. He did it about a month after that picture was taken."

Oh God. I wish I could undo this conversation, go back to the dreamy, wispy cloud I was floating on only moments before.

My shyness has been torn away by the revelations that passed between us. I reach out and take his hand, lace my fingers into the spaces between his. His hand grasps mine.

He sets his cup down and turns his head toward me. His breath is sweet despite the coffee, but it's laced with something else—something like sorrow. He presses his lips to my mouth.

Here's the thing about the kiss. It's full of everything I've been missing for so long. Connection. Understanding. Warmth. And it rushes through me so fast, I feel like I'm drowning. I can't breathe. Without thinking, I push him away. His eyes fill with hurt.

Immediately, I regret it. I open my mouth to apologize, but he's already standing up.

"I've gotta go."

He's gone before I can protest. I melt onto the couch, gasping, realizing I've never wanted anything as much as I want to rewind time and return to that kiss. And it scares me. The fact that something so beautiful and tenuous is within my grasp terrifies me because I know that, at some point, I will just end up losing it.

Hours later, I flip through the channels, trying to find something interesting enough to keep me awake until Mattie gets home. I should go upstairs and find my caffeine pills, but I feel stuck, like I've been glued to the couch. It would take way too much energy to climb the stairs. No, I'll just sit here and watch TV and wait.

Hoarders? No.

Full House? No.

The Real World? NO.

I settle on the Science Channel. There's some program about how the world is going to end soon, and it kind of cheers me up because then at least I won't be sliced to bits by Sophie's killer. The show's narrator has such a soothing voice. I find myself succumbing to the sleep I've been staving off for so long. Finally, I just give in.

And promptly slide.

Black leather. The vibrations of a running engine travel up my legs and into my spine. I recognize the unmistakable mixture of gasoline and orange shampoo.

Scotch.

But I don't think I'm *inside* Scotch. No. Whoever I've become is sitting in the passenger seat, rubbing her earlobe between her thumb and forefinger. When I realize the girl is missing an earring, I put two and two together. Amber. The damn earring I picked up in the bathroom must have poked through my jeans and touched my thigh.

When Amber turns her head, I see Scotch staring out the windshield into nothingness. The view stretches on for miles and miles. Angled roofs and shedding trees and glowing streetlights. I've been here before, to Lookout Peak. Rollins and I came here the one and only time I smoked pot. We were a total cliché, lying on the hood of his car, staring at the stars and wondering if there was something, anything else out there in the big, starry sky.

"You can't tell anyone," Scotch says.

It seems I've come into the middle of a conversation.

"It was just the one time. We used protection." Desperation tinges Scotch's voice, and I'm sure he's talking about the pregnancy. "The baby probably wasn't even mine. Samantha said she saw Sophie riding around with Mr. Golden after school. Who knows how many guys she was sleeping with?"

Finally, Amber speaks. "When did you find out about the pregnancy?"

"Last week. Before . . ." He doesn't finish his sentence, just takes a swig from a bottle he's been holding between his knees.

Fresh tears spill down Amber's cheeks. I wonder how she ended up here, in Scotch's car, parked at Lookout Peak. Did she run into him after the funeral? Did he ask her if she wanted to go for a ride? My guess is they were two comets traveling at high velocities when they came crashing together—Scotch drunk, and Amber needing someone to just be with her.

"Do you think that's why she did it?" Amber asks.

Scotch beats his hand on the steering wheel. "I don't know. At first, she talked about taking care of it, going somewhere. But then she said she didn't know if she could go through with it. She just should've gotten rid of it."

I wish I could climb into his brain and pick apart his thoughts. When Sophie told him about the pregnancy, did he panic? Did he insist she get an abortion? Did she refuse?

Even if I did manage to slide into Scotch, I wouldn't be able to read his thoughts. That's not the way sliding works. I'd only see the world from his perspective, and that is *not* an attractive possibility for me.

Amber crosses her arms over her stomach and rocks back and forth.

"It would have ruined my plans. It would have ruined my life."

Scotch takes another pull off the bottle and then shakes his head like it burns going down. He leans toward Amber and starts to nuzzle her neck. She exhales, a cross between a sigh and a moan. When his hand slithers into her lap, I realize where this is going. Memories come rushing back, and instead of being inside the cramped front seat of a Mustang, I'm lying on a bench in the boys' locker room. As Scotch touches Amber, I feel sick, like I'm witnessing exactly what he did to me that night. It is so, so messed up.

Amber's body responds to Scotch's caresses, and she

leans toward him. I'm no longer worried for her safety. I'm worried about my own sanity. If I stay here while they do this, I will surely go insane. Slowly, I feel myself slipping away.

Relief rushes through me when I realize I'm back in my own living room. My heart is thumping hard inside my rib cage, and the memories of the homecoming dance last year are rattling my brain. Instead of the program about the impending apocalypse, there's a show about the mating ritual of the baboon. I grab the remote and turn the television off, shuddering.

I take the steps two at a time, unable to get to my room fast enough. Unable to get to my *pills* fast enough. I snatch up my backpack and thrust my hand inside, searching for the familiar curve of the bottle. The childproof top comes off with a twist, and then the white ovals are in my palm, and then they are in my mouth. I swallow them without water, without hesitation.

Only when I feel them sliding down my throat does my heart slow to a normal rhythm. I vow not to let my guard down again. When my body sinks into the looseness of sleep, I leave myself unprotected. I'd rather not sleep at all than to be sucked into the presence of would-be rapists. Of killers.

All that night, I lie on my bed and watch old episodes of *Buffy the Vampire Slayer* on Netflix. I imagine myself with a stake, chasing after a shadowy figure in a mask carrying a knife wet with Sophie's blood. I tackle him to the ground and rip away the material obscuring his face. It is Scotch. I raise the stake high and plunge it deep into his chest. He disintegrates like dust and is swallowed up by the earth.

CHAPTER FOURTEEN

In the morning, I take an eternity-long shower, trying to scrub away any remaining bit of Scotch with my vanilla body wash. I'd probably stand here all day, letting the warm water cascade over my body, if my sister didn't scream at me to hurry the hell up. I wrap myself in a frayed brown towel and open the door.

"It's about freaking time," she says. I ignore her and go into my room, pull on some faded jeans and a Minnie Mouse T-shirt, and wrangle a comb through the pink mop on my head, uttering a chain of obscenities. Before me, in the mirror, a girl stares at me with circles under her eyes.

In the kitchen, I find a note from my father: *Early meeting. See you tonight.* I have to admit, I'm a little relieved to miss him. He'd notice the circles and demand to know if I've been taking my Provigil like a good little narcoleptic, and I'm not sure I'd have the strength to lie.

I'm grabbing a brown sugar cinnamon Pop-Tart and stuffing it into my bag when, through the kitchen window,

I see Samantha pull up. Mattie rushes in, grabs a mottled banana, and bolts out, yelling something about being late for practice. Tires squeal as Samantha pulls away.

If I'm going to walk, I'd better hurry up, too. I grab my purple coat from the coat-tree in the front hall and wiggle into it before hurrying out the door.

In my driveway, Zane leans against a white Grand Am. His blond hair is all over the place, and he looks like he hasn't slept.

"Hi," I say, suddenly self-conscious about my appearance. I wish I'd spent some time putting on makeup. At least some concealer to cover the darkness under my eyes.

"Hey. I thought you might need a ride. You don't have a car, right?" His gaze sweeps the driveway.

"No." I plod down the driveway toward him. "I mean, no, I don't have a car. So a ride would be really nice. Thanks."

He holds the door for me and then circles around to the driver's side. My feet brush against crumpled Big Gulp cups and Snickers wrappers. When he turns the key in the ignition, a Nirvana song nearly pops my eardrums. He spins the knob to the left until the song blasts at a more acceptable level.

"Sorry."

"I'm sorry, too," I blurt out, then clamp my hand over my mouth. *Idiot.*

"For what?" He looks bewildered.

"For pushing you away. I was just surprised, that's all."

He stares into his lap. "Well, I shouldn't have kissed

you. We barely know each other." He backs out of my driveway, pausing to glance both ways before pulling into the street.

I want to say the kiss wasn't a mistake. I want to tell him I enjoyed it. I want to tell him I like him so much it terrifies me. Instead, I say, "So, you're into Nirvana?"

"Oh, yeah. Kurt Cobain is, like, my idol."

"Except for the whole killing-himself thing, right?"

I mean it to be a joke, but then I remember about his father.

"Oh my God. I'm so sorry. I didn't mean . . ." My voice trails off.

We're both quiet for the five minutes it takes to get to school. Kurt Cobain carries on the conversation for us.

We make it to English about thirty seconds before the bell rings. There's something odd about the room. I realize what's strange—Mrs. Winger is standing at the front of the room, smiling at everyone, ready to start the day, rather than huddled in front of her computer playing solitaire.

She's excited about something. She squawks and waves her flabby arms as she explains our assignment. She feels we're in need of some healing after our heartbreaking loss. We need to talk about our feelings, get it all out— some hippy-dippy bullshit. We'll do it anonymously. She passes out green sheets of paper, each one with a code word written at the top. Mine is *yellow*. I sneak a look at my neighbors' papers. *Purple. Black.*

Really working herself up, Mrs. Winger babbles on about the importance of expressing ourselves. She wants us to write what we're feeling now, right this minute. She wants us to pour ourselves out onto the page. Mike Jones raises his hand and asks if "tired" counts as a feeling. She gives him her patented death stare and then continues with her ridiculous monologue.

After we've purged our thoughts and emotions, Mrs. Winger will collect the pages and mix them up. Then she'll randomly pass out the papers, and we'll each write a heartfelt, kind, human response. She has the code words, she warns, so don't even think about writing something mean. She crouches down by Zane's desk, and I hear her tell him that since he's new and didn't know Sophie, he can write about whatever strikes him.

She puts on some classical "writing" music and settles behind her desk, firing up her computer—probably to get some solid solitaire time in—and puts up her feet. We all quietly stare at our papers for a while. Finally, one by one, my classmates bend over their desks and start writing. Zane writes a word, then pauses, writes another. Samantha is hunched over her desk, scribbling furiously.

I'm the last one to begin. My pencil feels strange and hard and it kind of hurts to hold on to. I realize it's because I'm squeezing it so tightly. What do I have to say about Sophie? What am I feeling?

Sophie was one of the nicest people I've ever known.

I pause. It seems wrong to just leave it at *nice. Nice* is what you say when a stranger asks about your weekend and you don't really want to go into it. *Nice* is the weather. It means nothing. Nothing at all.

What do I really have to say about Sophie?

I chew on my eraser. This *is* anonymous, after all. I flip over my pencil and rub out the part about her being nice.

Sophie was a beautiful person, inside and out, but everyone treated her like crap. The girls she called "friends" only accepted her when she was skinny. The guy she liked screwed her over. There is more to Sophie's death than you'll ever know.

Before I can write more, Mrs. Winger is at the front of the room, announcing, "Time's up! Fold your papers and turn them in!" I press my paper neatly in half and pass it forward. Once Mrs. Winger has collected all the papers, she shuffles them and then weaves among the desks, giving them to new people.

She flips a paper onto my desk. I don't touch it.

When she's finished, she gestures for us to unfold the papers. "Read and respond," she says. "Really connect with each other."

Teachers are so lame. They think they can make us bare our souls through some stupid activity in class. If social boundaries can keep a jock from saying *what's up* to a nerd in the hallway, does she really think in one period she can make us best friends like the kids in *The Breakfast Club*? I roll my eyes and unfold my paper.

There's this girl. And I'm pretty sure I like her. I mean, I know I do, but the thing is, I don't know how to tell her. I don't really know the protocol for this sort of thing. So yeah. I guess that's all. If you have some advice, it would be greatly appreciated.

I steal a look at Zane. It has to be his. No one else was told to just write about whatever. Is it vain to think he could be writing about me? I remember how his lips felt on mine, so warm and sudden. I wish I could go back to that moment, go with the flow, not ruin it.

"Two-minute warning!" Mrs. Winger is already dancing around, trying to hurry us. Shit. What to say?

Quickly, I jot down, *Tell her she's so pretty it kills you a little.*

Then I refold the piece of paper and push it into Mrs. Winger's waiting hands. She collects the rest of the papers and then starts unfolding them and handing them back according to the code words at the top. I watch Zane open his. He smiles.

She places my paper in front of me. I skim past my original note and read the response: *Uh, I think you're reading too much into this. Girl had problems. She took the easy way out. Done.* I glance around the room. Samantha is watching me carefully. I slowly crumple the piece of paper, holding her gaze the whole time. She looks away.

The bell rings. Zane pauses by my desk, waiting for me to gather my things. On the way out the door, I toss the paper into the garbage can. Zane says something about Mrs. Winger literally having wings when she waves her arms around, and I'm laughing as we turn the corner and enter the hallway.

I catch sight of Rollins, halfway down the hall, heading in our direction, probably to meet up with me. He blinks when he sees me with Zane, and looks a little hurt. I try to smile and wave, but he ducks into a bathroom. My hand flutters uselessly down by my side.

Everyone stares as I walk down the hall with Zane. It's probably partly because Zane is the New Kid, and there's always a bit of mystery shrouding the New Kid, but mostly it's because he is smoking hot. I savor the look of jealousy I get when we pass by a bunch of freshman girls.

Zane stops at the drinking fountain to fill his green Nalgene bottle, and I wait, shifting my books from one hip to the other. The hallway hollows out by the second, people rushing to class before the bell rings.

"What do you have next?" I ask when he straightens.

"Government with Carson. Guess I could use a nap."

Mr. Carson has to be over a hundred years old. He's been teaching here since our school opened in the 1950s. His idea of a lesson plan is ordering you to copy five pages of messily scrawled notes from the overhead, lulling you into a nearly comatose state, and then scaring you to death by hacking up a lung into a purple hanky right when you least expect it. Every year, people place bets on whether this'll be his last.

"Oh, come on. His class is *scintillating.*" I stress the cheap SAT vocabulary word, and Zane laughs. The sound heats me up.

All morning, I've been imagining Zane's lips pressed to mine, like the image of us kissing is superimposed on reality. We're just standing here in the hallway chatting, but in my head our limbs are wrapped around each other, our bodies doing the talking.

The bell rings, threatening reality. I want to escape into an alternate universe, one where I get to make out with Zane beneath the bleachers instead of wondering who killed Sophie Jacobs. Suddenly I understand the presence of that condom wrapper I saw under the bleachers last week. It was evidence of someone breaking away from the homework and lockers and lunch ladies— someone fleeing a world that lets a girl disappear and doesn't ask questions.

"Do you want to skip?" I ask, and the question is so out of nowhere it even surprises *me*.

"And go where?"

"I know a place."

Zane smiles. He doesn't know that *he* is my refuge, the place I will go to escape.

It's colder this week. The wind whooshes beneath the bleachers, cutting through the thin material of my T-shirt. I should have thought out this plan better, brought my coat or something. But then Zane shrugs out of one side of his oversized corduroy coat, offering to let me share it with him, and I think everything is perfect.

"So this is your place?" He looks around him, taking it all in. The candy bar wrappers. The cigarette butts. The mounds of dead leaves.

"It's not much," I say. "But yeah. It's where I go."

Zane nods. "It's got a certain . . . mystique to it."

Mystique. Just the word to describe a place where you

can see but can't be seen, where you hear the things you don't want to know. Just then, I realize why I'm so comfortable under the bleachers. Me lurking down here, it's just like me sliding. I am a witness. Never a participant.

"Something on your mind?" Zane asks, bumping into me playfully.

There is actually something on my mind. I keep replaying the conversation I heard between Scotch and Amber. The thing he'd said about a pregnancy ruining his life—would he go so far as to kill Sophie if she didn't get an abortion? Is that too far-fetched?

I feel like I need a new perspective. I could tell Zane the basics without revealing my secret. Maybe he'll have some insight.

"Okay, you know the girl who died? Sophie?"

Zane nods.

"Well, this officer came to our house, asking my sister questions about Sophie's state of mind. He happened to mention Sophie was pregnant when she died."

"Holy shit."

"Yeah. Anyway . . . I think I might know who the father was. You know Scotch Becker?"

Zane groans. "Who could forget a guy named Scotch? He's the charming fellow who suggested I go out for football. He said I seemed cool enough to get some of his castoffs."

I pause, the statement hitting a little close to home. "Gross. Okay, so the day Sophie died, I overheard Scotch telling one of his friends that he slept with Sophie."

Zane stares straight ahead. "That just . . . sucks."

I follow his gaze to the empty field. It's easier to look at nothing when talking about these things than to look into Zane's eyes and try to guess what he's thinking. What I'm about to say might derail everything that's happened between us in the past few days. Maybe he'll think I'm crazy, paranoid like Samantha's note in English class said.

But maybe not.

"Okay, so is it totally insane to think Sophie might not have killed herself?" I continue to not look at Zane. Instead, I pick up an orangey-brown leaf and start to shred it.

A moment passes.

"Um. What do you mean? If she didn't kill herself, then who killed her?"

Another moment.

"You think Scotch killed her? Because of the pregnancy? That he killed her and made it look like a suicide?" His voice sounds doubtful, but not like he thinks the idea is so out there I must be destined for a padded cell.

"It's a theory," I say diplomatically. "Hey, Scott Peterson killed his wife when she was pregnant. And they were married. Scotch had a lot to lose. He'd probably have to give up football and get a job at a car dealership or something. He'd never get out of Iowa."

Zane hunches forward and rubs his chin thoughtfully. "Yeah, I guess. Still, it seems like a big assumption—that he'd kill a girl over something like that."

I could tell Zane about what Scotch did to me freshman

year. If I do, though, it's like it turns me into Damaged Girl, and I don't want that. I decide to shoot a different theory his way.

"Okay, here's another possibility. Kids have been talking about Sophie riding around with Mr. Golden. What if he's the father? That would definitely be a motive to kill Sophie, wouldn't it? His job would be at stake. He could go to jail for sleeping with a minor. But if he took her out and made it look like she killed herself, he'd be off the hook."

Zane twists his mouth, like he's considering his words carefully. "Maaaaaaybe. Or maybe she just killed herself, Sylvia. I mean, that's what people do when they feel like there's no escape."

I feel the weight of his father's suicide hanging between us. Zane, more than anyone, would know how each day could burden someone so much that they'd want to take their own life. The thing is, he didn't know Sophie. If he did, maybe he'd be more willing to think outside the box.

"I'm not saying you're wrong, Sylvia. I'm just saying that, when it comes to these things, the least complicated explanation is usually right. Sophie was pregnant. She didn't know what to do. She was probably scared. She felt like she had no way out. Sounds like a recipe for disaster to me."

I have to admit, he makes a good point.

We are quiet for a while, and I just let the heat from his body seep into mine. Sharing his coat reminds me of when Rollins and I pretended to be Siamese twins. Except when

I was with Rollins, my heart didn't feel like it was going to slam its way right out of my chest.

I hear a faraway bell. The period has ended. It's time to return to my own personal hell, high school. Zane slips his half of the coat off and puts it around my shoulder, fully enveloping me with warmth.

"Come on," he says. "And try to avoid the broken glass. Can't have you going to the nurse and meeting some other guy."

CHAPTER FIFTEEN

Zane and I mix with the stream of students flowing down the hallway. Someone catches my elbow, and I turn to see a blond cheerleader I used to be sort of friends with. Her eyes are bright, and she's bubbling with excitement.

"You missed it. Mattie and Amber got into a fight!"

"What?"

"Just now. Mattie called Amber a slut, so Amber punched her. It was. So. Insane." The girl breaks away from me and launches herself toward someone else to broadcast the latest news.

"What's wrong?" Zane asks when he sees how white my face has become.

"It's my sister. Jesus, I've gotta find her. I'll talk to you later."

"Sure, no problem. See you." He squeezes my hand and then disappears into the crowd of people. I stand on my tippy-toes and survey the masses on their way to class, frantically searching for my sister's face. She's nowhere to be seen. I let the flow of bodies carry me down the hallway, passing classrooms and drinking fountains. As we go by the office, I spot Mattie through the window.

Mattie and Amber sit outside the principal's office, only one tacky orange chair between them. They avoid looking at each other, grimacing at their laps. My sister's clothes are disheveled, the neckline of her cheerleading uniform ripped.

Nasty emerges from his office. His mouth makes shapes and his finger points as he speaks, but I can't hear him behind the smudgy window. He says something to my sister and then waves her out of his office like he's tired of seeing her.

She bursts through the door and almost slams right into me. "Vee!"

I steer her toward the girls' bathroom by her elbow. A senior in ridiculously high heels stands before a mirror, coaxing a contact lens back into place. She blinks a few times, picks up her pink purse from the counter, and brushes past us on her way out. All the stalls are empty, so I'm free to WTF all I want.

"What happened?" I demand, crossing my arms over my chest.

Promptly Mattie bursts into tears. "Amber's such a bitch. She said Scotch knocked Sophie up and that's why she killed herself."

I let out a deep breath. "She said that?"

Mattie ducks into a stall and starts unrolling toilet paper. She dabs at her cheeks, wiping away the mascara streams coursing down her face. "Yeah, well, we were at my locker, and Samantha made some comment about Amber taking off with Scotch after the funeral. Amber hinted that he told her something big, and we kind of pushed her into telling us."

"And then she hit you?"

Mattie shakes her head. "No. Amber said that's why Sophie must have killed herself—because of the pregnancy. I got pissed because it's like she was excusing herself from any responsibility. I mean, after what we did . . . So I asked her if she'd already forgotten about the picture she sent everyone, if she really thought that had nothing to do with Sophie's suicide. That's when she punched me."

Mattie dissolves into tears. I can't stand the way she's crying, knowing she blames herself for Sophie's death. I want so badly to tell her that, although Sophie was unbearably hurt by her friends' actions, she didn't kill herself. I can't bring myself to tell her the truth, and I hate myself for it.

Instead, I pull her close and wrap my arms around her. "Mattie, you can't blame yourself or Amber for Sophie's death. There were other factors involved. Trust me. If you want to feel bad about making a mistake, go ahead, but make it a productive feeling. Don't do anything like that again. But you *can't* go around thinking Sophie is dead because of you."

Mattie pulls away slightly and looks me in the eyes. "Are you sure?"

"Of course I am, Mattie. I swear. You have to trust me."

She leans her head on my shoulder and sniffles. "I do."

After a moment, she pulls away and goes to the sink. She splashes water on her face and then smooths her hair. Meeting my gaze in the mirror, she offers a small smile. "Thanks, Vee."

"No problem. So what did Nasty say?"

"He went easy on me because of Sophie's death. He said he knew I was going through a lot, so he only gave me three days of in-school suspension. I'm supposed to go around and get stuff to work on."

In-school suspension is so *not* a big deal. Kids call it lockup, ironically. You have to sit in a little room attached to the teachers' lounge and listen to the teachers gossip about who cheated on the *Macbeth* final exam. There's a pop machine right outside the door, and if you play your cards right, you can nab a can of soda to make your stay more enjoyable. Not that I would know or anything.

Mattie's skin is all blotchy, and her eyes are red and puffy. A red welt is forming on her cheek, where I assume Amber hit her. She looks like she's about to start crying again any minute.

"Look, do you want me to go around and get your assignments for you?"

"Would you?" she asks hopefully. "I don't want anyone to see me."

"Sure. I'm not exactly in the mood for class." To be completely truthful, I'm not exactly in the mood to run into Rollins after he snubbed me this morning.

She pounces on me. "You're the best!"

I walk her to the teachers' lounge. The window is covered in newspaper—probably so we can't see the teachers partying during their prep periods. Mattie waves and ducks into the lounge. After she disappears, I try to figure out which of her classes to go to first. I decide to hit up her English class, since it's the closest. Her teacher isn't all that excited that I interrupted class, but she finds a *Romeo and Juliet* study guide and shoves it my way. Mattie's other teachers are more pleasant and give me some worksheets to pass on to her.

Next, I stop by her locker to get her textbooks. You can open 97.3 percent of the lockers at East High by punching them in just the right spot, so you learn really quickly to carry all valuables with you. Mattie's locker, which she shared with Sophie, is a disaster. Photos are taped haphazardly on the inside of the door, among scribbled messages saying things like *Scotch is hawt* and *Mattie + Sophie = BFFEE* (Best Friends For-Effing-Ever).

My eyes fall on one picture in the center of everything, the eye of the storm. Mattie stands between Sophie and Amber, and their arms are all around each other's waists. From the way their faces are painted like cats, I can tell it's from the state fair last summer. It seems like the picture was taken a million years ago. One of the girls is now dead, and the other two just mauled each other in the hallway. It reminds me how quickly things can change.

On the bottom of her locker, under her gym shoes, which smell like rotting broccoli, under a bunch of flyers advertising the cheerleaders' car· wash from September, under something suspiciously slimy in a paper bag, I find Mattie's English textbook. I shake my head and pull it out, feeling a bit like the magician who snatches a tablecloth out from under a bunch of china.

As I straighten up, I see Amber headed my way. Her hair hangs in long, messy clumps, and it's pretty clear she's been crying. It's actually really sad. Between witnessing her crumpled on the bathroom floor of a funeral home and then later making out with Scotch Becker, the lowest of the low, I only feel pity for her.

She stops at her locker and spins the knob. When she tries to pull the locker open, nothing happens. She tries again. And again. The locker stays shut. Finally, she releases a shriek and pounds on the metal before drooping in defeat.

"Amber?"

She turns her miserable face toward me.

"Are you okay? Do you want some help?"

She laughs bitterly. "I want a lot of things. Can you turn back time for me? Because that'd be great. I could go back and not be such an idiot. Not send that picture to everyone. Not be such a slut. Not get into a huge fight with my best friend." She shakes her head.

"I meant with your locker." I push past her gently and pound on the door in just the right spot. It pops open.

"Thanks," she mutters, and pulls out her backpack. She shrugs it over her shoulders and slams the locker door. "Guess I'll see ya later."

I watch her walk down the hallway and disappear around the corner.

Maybe I've been wrong about Amber all along. Beneath that cold, bitchy exterior, it seems like she's actually pretty vulnerable. She's able to see the error of her ways, at least, and that's more than you can say for some people. Once Mattie's cooled off, I vow to put in a good word for Amber. They can help each other get past Sophie's death.

Armed with the English textbook and worksheets, I head toward the teachers' lounge. In the detention room, Mattie is sitting with her back to the door, her head cradled in her arms. At first, I wonder if she's crying, but when I touch her back and she turns toward me, her eyes are clear.

I set the work sheets and textbook on the desk in front of her.

"Thanks," she says.

"No problem," I reply. "You'd do the same for me." In my head, though, I'm wondering if it's true.

When I turn to leave, Mattie grabs my arm.

"No, really," she says. "I appreciate you being here for me. I know we haven't always gotten along . . ."

"Don't worry about it. That's what I'm here for." I mean what I say, but as I turn to leave, I find myself wondering who *I'm* supposed to count on.

CHAPTER SIXTEEN

After school, I fight my way through the crowd to get to my locker. It seems like everyone is yapping about the fight. I wish I had earplugs so I could stop hearing all the gossip about my sister and Amber.

Just as I'm stuffing an orange notebook into the already-bursting seams of my poor bag, Rollins appears. He leans on the locker next to mine.

"Hey. I heard about your sister. That sucks."

I give him a cold look. There's something about him ignoring me this morning and now trying to act all buddy-buddy with me that rubs me the wrong way.

"So we're friends now? Because I wasn't sure after this morning. . . ."

"What are you talking about?" Rollins tries to look innocent. It's infuriating.

I feel like everything from the last couple of days is building up inside me, a crescendo of terror and anger and frustration. The need for release is so strong.

I turn to face him. "Let's review. You walk out on Friday

night for no reason. When my sister's best friend dies, you don't call. You don't text. Nothing. And now you're avoiding me in the halls. Oh, yeah. I saw you this morning. As soon as you realized I was with Zane, you turned and walked away. Let me tell you something, Rollins. I need a friend right now. Get it?"

A muscle in his jaw twitches. He doesn't say a word, just does a 180 and walks the other way, his fists clenching and unclenching.

"What was that all about?"

Zane pops out of nowhere and stoops to rest his arm on my open locker door. His grin is a mile wide—so bright and warm, I can almost feel the sun beating down on my face.

"Nothing," I mutter. "I'm just having a really heinous day."

"Hmmm," he says, pressing one finger against his chin like he's thinking hard. "There's only one thing that makes me feel better when I'm having a bad day. Jelly doughnuts."

"What?" My stony face cracks into a smile.

"Jelly doughnuts. They're like an instant orgasm for your tongue. Come on, we'll go get some. I know the best place."

I slam my locker door and let him lead me down the hall toward the parking lot.

An hour and 89,467 calories later, we pull into my driveway. I'm still licking the cherry goodness from my fingers, sighing from the clump of sugar in my belly. The air in the car is sweet and comfortably warm.

"Can I ask you a question?" Zane says, playing with the radio. He puts on some bad eighties music. It's perfect.

"Go for it."

"You and Rollins, you're tight?"

"We're friends," I say, and then start to feel pretty guilty about blowing up at Rollins. To make up for it, I add, "*Best* friends."

Zane absorbs this information. "I keep thinking about yesterday." His hand is on the armrest between us, not far away from my bare arm. Goose bumps. "I'm sorry I kissed you so soon. I feel like I ruined everything. I mean, I think you're really interesting. I'd like to get to know you better."

A feeling like happiness swirls beneath my skin. He wants to get to know me better. That means he doesn't think I'm a crazy bitch for throwing out those murder theories, right? That means he feels this connection, too.

"It's just a really weird time for me," I say finally. "With this whole Sophie thing and my sister freaking out. I feel like I'm stuck in this nightmare and everyone's insane but me. Or maybe I'm the one who's insane. I don't know."

Shut up, Vee. Shut up. You're babbling.

After a while, he says softly, "I had a little sister once."

We are both quiet. Even though the heater is blasting hot air right in my face, I feel cold from the tips of my toes to the top of my scalp. The way he said it, in past tense, makes me feel like crying.

"I'm sorry," I say, and then I wish I had said something else, anything else. "Do you want to talk about it?"

He squeezes his eyes shut and shakes his head.

The white bag I'm holding between my thighs crinkles as I pull out a pastry. "Jelly doughnut?"

Our eyes meet, and he shines his smile again. It warms me up fast. His fingers brush mine as he takes the doughnut from me. He takes a big bite, chews, swallows.

"God," he says. "You're so beautiful. It just kills me."

"It was you," I whisper. "In class, I mean. That *was* your note."

His lips bend into a smile.

The moment freezes. And right now, I don't care if this will end someday. My fear of becoming too attached is swept away by my intense desire to make this instant count, make it as complete as it can be.

My hand floats up to his face and touches his cheek. Leaning toward each other, we kiss, ever so gently. His lips taste like cherry. I didn't know it could be this good.

When I manage to extricate myself from Zane's car, I notice my dad's car is in the driveway—an odd sight in the late afternoon. I thought he was going to be at the hospital, catching up on some paperwork.

Once inside, I set down my backpack and head to the kitchen to get a drink of water. A strange sound makes me pause in the middle of the foyer. It's a rustling—no, it's someone whispering. The noise is coming from my father's study. I inch closer, straining to hear what's being said.

"Just stop," my father hisses loudly. "I told you. Please don't call anymore." A moment passes, and then he says,

"No. I'm done. Good-bye."

I'm frozen. I know I should turn around, go to the kitchen for a glass of water like I planned, but my muscles will not obey my command. Who could my father have been talking to? It sounded like he was putting an end to some sort of relationship. But he hasn't gone out on any dates . . . has he?

My father appears in the doorway with his cell phone, and his face looks older than it normally does. Deep creases carve into his face around his eyes and mouth. His back is hunched over. He looks up, surprised to see me.

"Vee," he says. "How long have you been standing there?"

I shrug, trying to appear casual. "Not long."

He slips his cell phone into his pocket and grabs his jacket. "I've got to run to the store for a few things. You need me to pick anything up?"

"No," I say.

"Okay. I won't be long."

And then he's gone.

I linger in the doorway of his office, trying to make sense of the phone call I overheard. I have to admit, I kind of always pictured my dad staying single for the rest of his life. It had never occurred to me that he'd want to see anyone after my mom died.

On his desk, a framed photo of my mother grabs my attention. It's from their wedding. In it, she smiles widely at the camera, as if she's got her whole life ahead of her, as if nothing bad could ever happen. As if she could never die, as if my father could never love anyone but her.

Looking at it makes me feel heavy with sadness. Only moments ago, I was kissing a gorgeous boy, maybe even falling a little bit in love. I was throwing caution to the wind, letting myself get stuck to something. But right now, in front of me, is the evidence that all good things, no matter how beautiful, do come to an end.

I turn around and trudge up the stairs, my heart weighing me down.

CHAPTER SEVENTEEN

Dinner is awkward.

Mattie sits there, twisting her spoon in her hands, avoiding eye contact with my dad. He fills our bowls with steaming chili and places them in front of us silently. The chili is his way of making amends for not being around while Mattie's dealing with her best friend's death and for relying on me to pick up the slack. I also wonder if he's making up for something else, maybe for not being entirely truthful with us. For keeping his relationship with whoever was on the phone earlier on the down-low.

He reaches across the table for some saltines to crumble into his chili and then asks casually—almost *too* casually, "So what happened with Amber today, Mattie?"

Mattie stares intently at the spoon in her fist.

"She was saying some stuff about Sophie."

"What *kind* of stuff?" He takes a bite, chews methodically, never looking away from Mattie's face.

After a long pause, Mattie says, "She was saying Sophie was pregnant with Scotch Becker's baby."

My father swallows, frowns. "And why would that upset you?"

Mattie drums her spoon on the table. "Because she said that's why Sophie killed herself, and I know that's not true."

"So you hit her?"

Mattie lets her spoon fall to the table. "I didn't hit her! She hit me. I just called her a name. I shouldn't have been *suspended* for that."

My dad keeps his cool. "Well, Mr. Nast can't just allow kids to get into brawls in the hallway. He has a school to run. There have to be consequences, even if—"

"Even if what?" Mattie says, challenging him.

"Even if you're hurting."

Mattie lets out a long breath. "You have *no* idea." She then picks up her untouched bowl of chili and heads for the kitchen. I hear the dish hit the sink with a great deal of force. My dad winces.

"I'm going to bed," Mattie announces on her way back through the dining room. She stomps up the stairs and slams her bedroom door.

My dad sighs and puts his head in his hands.

I desperately want to follow Mattie's lead and bow out of this whole depressing family meal, but it seems cruel to let my father sit there by himself. When he raises his head, I see tears glistening in his eyes.

"I can't do this by myself," he says, more to the ceiling than to me. I'm not sure how to respond. I'm not sure if I *should* respond.

"God. If only your mother were here," he goes on. "I'm

just . . . unequipped. I can't deal with this."

His yearning for my mother sinks into me. In that moment, I almost wish he *was* seeing someone. He needs someone in his life besides me and Mattie—someone to talk to.

I reach over and link my hand with his. "You're doing fine, Dad. Mattie's just upset. She'll be okay." I hope what I'm saying isn't a lie.

He looks at our hands, intertwined, and a tear comes loose and spills down his cheek. He squeezes my hand and attempts a smile. "You remind me so much of your mother sometimes, Vee. She always knew just what to say. It was like she could look inside of you and know exactly what you were feeling. You're like that."

His words make me a little uncomfortable. Usually I feel like I know *too much* about other people—their secrets eat away at me from the inside.

"Vee. Would you do me a favor? Go to your sister. She needs help. You probably understand what she's going through more than I ever could. You'll know the right things to say."

I manage a small smile. "Sure, Dad."

My father's phone buzzes. He pulls it out of his pocket, glances at the display, and answers it. "Hello?" As I watch, his eyes dry up and become businesslike. "No problem. I'll be there in a half hour."

He hangs up and looks at me. "I'm sorry, Vee. I have to go."

"I know," I reply. "Go."

Upstairs, Mattie is lying on her bed, flipping through a photo album of happier times. On one page, my mother pushes me on a swing, and my sister is visible in the background, strapped into a pink stroller. She's reaching her arms out, like she longs to join in on the fun. The next page shows my mom and dad cooking dinner together. I am dancing between them, tasting something on a wooden spoon and making a face. She is stuck in her highchair, a mound of cereal on her tray.

I sit next to her on the bed, but she doesn't look up. She says her words to the people in the pictures. "What do you remember about her?" She traces her finger over our mother's smile.

"About Mom?"

Mattie nods. "I feel like I've forgotten everything important."

I flop back on the bed and stare at the ceiling. "I don't know. She smelled like violets. When we went on car trips, she made up stories about the constellations in the sky. They were like people to her. They all had pasts and relationships and mannerisms. She could go on for hours about the Gemini twins fighting over Andromeda."

Mattie turns the page. "What else?"

"She ate peanut butter and banana sandwiches. She played her music loud and jumped around. She painted her toenails purple."

Mattie examines each page in the photo album carefully, as if she's looking for clues about who our mother was. When she reaches the final page, it's blank. It's always been blank. I don't know what she was expecting. She hurls the book to the floor.

"It's not enough," she says, her words strangled by her sobs.

I sit up and wrap my arms around her. "I know," I whisper. "I know it's not enough. But listen. We've got each other. If you need to talk about something, you can tell me. Anything, okay?"

Mattie nods and grabs a tissue from her bedside table. I rub her back as she blows her nose. The light outside has gone dim. We are surrounded by shadows.

Eventually, my sister pulls away and rearranges herself on the bed, hugging a pillow across her chest. "Can I ask you a question, Vee?"

"Yeah."

She picks some lint off the pillow. "Why did you stop being friends with Sam and all those guys?"

I sigh. I'd been content to let Mattie think the popular crowd rejected me just for being a geek, but the way she looks at me makes me want to tell her the truth—or at least as much of it as I can. Besides, she should know what the people she hangs around with are capable of. Maybe it will save her from putting herself in the same situation I did.

"Do you remember the purple dress?" I ask.

She bobs her head excitedly, like I knew she would. She was there when I found the dress. She was almost more excited about it than I was.

And so I tell her.

I tell her about me and Samantha both liking Scotch. I tell her I was the one he chose and about all the things Samantha did to punish me for that. I tell her about drinking in Kapler Park before the dance. I tell her about how I felt ill and passed out, and how I awoke with my dress around my waist, to the sound of Rollins's fists hitting Scotch's body.

The only part I leave out is the sliding, but let's face it—it's not necessary to the story. What happened that night could happen to anyone. It is not a unique tale. But it is enough to cause my sister's face to screw up again with tears, enough to compel her to throw her arms around me and crush me with her embrace.

It's been a long time since I cried about that night. But for some reason, telling it all to Mattie, I see it from a different angle. My heart swells for the girl in the purple dress, for the girl with a crush who got more than she asked for. As I recall seeing it from Samantha's eyes—Scotch dragging me into the locker room—I start to cry for the girl I once was.

And so I let my sister hug me, and when she asks me to stay in her room tonight, I oblige. It's like when we were little, after our mom died, and she had a nightmare. She'd come into my room, and I'd hold up the covers for her to crawl under.

I watch her face as it settles into sleep. She looks so young, so raw. I'm angry for her that she didn't have more time with our mother, that the only person she really has right now is me. These thoughts circle over my head, and before I know it, I have fallen asleep.

I'm in the middle of a carnival. A Ferris wheel spins backward and a sad clown holds a bunch of black balloons. My mother rides a purple unicorn on the merry-go-round. I see her coming my way, and she waves, her face glowing in excitement. She looks just like her pictures, young and stunning.

She looks like an angel.

I run up to the gate and press against it, calling for her. Someone taps me on the shoulder, and when I turn around, there she is. She wears ripped blue jeans and an Alice in Chains T-shirt.

"Vee," she says, her voice soft and shimmery. She pulls me to a bench, and we sit down, hands clasped. I rest my head against her shoulder, breathing in her mother scent of powder and violets and milk.

"Mom."

It feels good to say the word. I have so many things to ask her. How did she know she was in love with Dad? Did his kisses taste like jelly doughnuts? How do I carry on each day with the knowledge of the terrible things people are capable of? How do I help my sister work through the blackness of one friend's death and another friend's betrayal?

All my questions fall away when I look in her eyes, blue against the black sky.

She pushes my hair back from my face. "My baby."

"Yes. Yes, Mom." I can't stop saying it. "Mom."

Rain begins to fall, and each drop that slides down my mother's cheeks takes away a tiny bit of her. She hugs me one last time, and then the rain picks up and takes her away entirely. The rain takes away everything.

I am crying when I awake in Mattie's room. How unfair this is, to be given a mother for a few seconds in a dream, only to have her be taken away the moment I open my eyes. The pillow is wet with tears.

The alarm clock says it's a little past ten. I need to get up, do something that will keep me alert. I slither out of Mattie's bed and tiptoe to the hallway, leaving her door just slightly ajar.

In my room, I snap on the light, and brightness blinds me. A face captures my attention in the corner of the room, but when I look, I realize it's only the face of the angel on the Smashing Pumpkins T-shirt. I'd hung the shirt over the back of my rocking chair and forgotten it. Something about the angel's eyes, the expression on her face. It reminds me of my mother.

Drawn to the shirt, I thread my arms through the sleeves and pull it over my head. It's softer than it looks, but its caress on my skin is a poor substitute for my dream mother's embrace.

After popping a few caffeine pills, I retrieve the astronomy book from my nightstand. I flip it open to a random page and start reading about the big bang theory. After only a paragraph, the words start to swerve on the page.

Dizziness. A slight pain behind my eyes.

I'm going to slide.

And then I realize I'm wearing the shirt that Rollins gave me.

An entire field pops up around me—not a natural field, but a man-made field, complete with white paint marking the perimeters for playing football. I see the dark but unmistakable outline of the school. Beyond it, the black sky sings with stars.

Rollins crosses the field, heading in the direction of a goalpost. It is strange to be inside him. The way his body moves, his kind of slouchy walk, is so familiar to me—but I've never experienced it from this perspective. I don't know how I've avoided it in the year that I've known him. I used to think it was because he contained his feelings so well. He never left an emotional imprint on anything.

Except the T-shirt he gave me. How strange.

As he approaches the goalpost, I see the silhouette of someone waiting for him—a female silhouette. I'm surprised by a sudden pang of jealousy. I didn't know he was seeing anyone. Have we drifted so far apart that I wouldn't know these things?

The girl's hair shines in the dim light coming from the faraway streetlamp. I know only one girl whose hair is that exact shade of chocolate brown. It is Amber.

Confusion overwhelms me. Though Amber has never made her attraction to Rollins a secret, he always brushes her off. What is going on here?

When he's about five yards away, I hear him say, "Thanks for coming."

Amber smiles and reaches into the black-and-white Prada purse that's slung over her shoulder. She pulls out a crumply packet, but it's too dark for me to tell what it is.

"I'm glad you called. I was feeling a little lonely."

Rollins opens his mouth to respond, but I'm snatched away before I can hear what he says. I jolt upright and gasp for air. I pull off the Smashing Pumpkins T-shirt and chuck it on the floor.

My phone wakes me before dawn. I sit up, feeling blindly for it. I must have fallen asleep in the early morning hours, despite the handful of caffeine pills I gulped down before witnessing Rollins's meeting with Amber.

It's my dad's ringtone, the one he made me download last year when I was stressing about finals—"Don't Worry, Be Happy." I swear the song is more annoying than my alarm clock.

"Dad? It's like five thirty."

"Vee, I've got to talk to you."

And, with those words, I know something terrible has happened. It's the kind of thing you say to someone right before breaking bad news. Like telling a child there's no Santa Claus. Or their cat got run over by a semi.

Or something much, much worse.

I'm suddenly sitting up, crushing the phone against my ear.

"What is it?"

"Amber's parents called. She didn't come home last night. They wondered if she was with Mattie." There's more. I can tell by his tone of voice there's something he's not telling me.

"And?"

"Honey, Amber is dead." The stark finality of his words knocks the breath out of me.

I take a moment, struggling to find my voice, trying to remember the last time I saw Amber. It was at her locker. That was the last time I saw her with my *own* eyes.

But I was *with* her around ten p.m. last night.

Or, rather, Rollins was with her.

I switch the phone from one ear to the other.

"Mr. Golden heard the shot and found her body on the football field—isn't that your psychology teacher? Evidently he was at school, preparing lesson plans for the day. God knows why he was there so late. What teacher stays until ten o'clock? The police say . . . it looks like another suicide."

I'm willing to bet it wasn't a suicide. Just like Sophie's death wasn't a suicide.

"Vee, are you okay?" He's making sure I've got my shit together so I can take care of Mattie. What choice do I have? I have to be okay. I have to keep Mattie safe.

Two cheerleaders are dead. She could be next.

"I'll be home by tonight, okay? We've got a bad situation here. I need you to stay with Mattie until I get home. There's no school today. The police have cordoned off the area."

I picture it in my head—yellow tape stretched around the football field, waving in the wind. Chalk marking where the body was found. Can you use chalk on grass?

My father interrupts my thoughts. "Okay? Okay,

Vee? Can you handle that?"

I'm nodding, but he can't see it. "Yeah, okay, Dad. Should I tell her?"

I hear him release a deep breath. "I guess you'd better. Will you guys be okay today?" Guilt has crept into his voice. Another traumatic event that he won't be around for.

"Don't worry," I say, and his ringtone pops into my head. *Be happy.* "I'll take care of everything."

CHAPTER EIGHTEEN

In the kitchen, I mix pancake batter while thinking of what I'll say to Mattie. There seems no good way to tell her. I'm glad I'm not a doctor. My father must go through this all the time, searching his mind for the perfect words to break bad news. I wonder why he's not better at it. Maybe I should be thinking about what my mother would say if she were here.

I pour little circles of batter into a sizzling pan, then grab a handful of chocolate chips and drop them one by one into the pancakes. A knock at the front door startles me. I peer through the window and see Rollins standing on our porch. I freeze for a moment and then duck down before he can see me. It's not something I think about, just instinct. Try as I might, I can't come up with a way to explain how Amber died right after she met up with Rollins.

He knocks again. I close my eyes.

Go. Away.

After about five minutes, I pick myself up off the floor and peek out the window. The porch is empty. Rollins is gone. I heave a sigh of relief.

I scoop the pancakes onto a plate. I spend a long time standing in front of the refrigerator, looking at a picture of my mom when she was in college, tan and skinny and smiling, with blond hair and a white tank top. Below it, there's a picture of my sister at her eighth-grade graduation. Dad and I stand on either side of her, giving her double bunny ears. On any other fridge, this would look like a happy collage of memories, but on our fridge it's a mockery of what once was, what could have been. A happy family.

I pull the refrigerator door open and grab the syrup so I can drizzle it on my sister's pancakes, just the way she likes them.

I nudge Mattie's door open with my foot and carry in the tray of pancakes and orange slices. Now that I'm standing there, it seems silly, like pancakes could possibly soften the blow that another of her friends is dead. I'm acting just like my freaking dad. Taking a couple of steps backward, I rest the tray on the floor in the hall and then enter the room again. I will do this in my own way.

She's snoring, her eyelashes thick against her cheeks. The strangest urge creeps through me—to crawl into bed next to her, wrap my arms around her, feel her torso rise and fall with each breath. Instead, I open the curtains and let the sun shine in, hoping it will obliterate the darkness my news will bring.

"Mattie?" I sit down next to her, shaking her gently. "Mattie, wake up."

She opens one eye and studies me. Then she jerks

upright, throwing her princess-pink covers away from her body.

"What time is it? Oh my God, I'm going to be late for practice. What—do I smell pancakes? Is it Sunday?" She stares at me, confused.

"Mattie, I have something to tell you."

She freezes, a look of apprehension washing over her face. Her muscles tense, like she's bracing herself for the impact.

"There's no school today. Amber's dead." No euphemisms, just the bald, ugly words. I rip the Band-Aid off and wait for her to scream.

Mattie's shoulders droop, then her eyes. I see the knowledge working its way through every muscle group, as they all become slack. First her face. Then her arms. Then the trunk of her body. She slumps there, devoid of any expression at all.

"They found her on the football field. They think it was suicide." Even as I'm speaking, I'm not entirely sure who *they* are. I have a vague mental picture of Officer Teahen and a bunch of uniformed figures inching their way across the campus, looking for clues.

Mattie says nothing.

I'm afraid to leave her alone, so I go into my room and grab some CDs and my old teddy bear, Cleo. I pop my Smashing Pumpkins CD into Mattie's computer because that's what I like to listen to when I feel as if my life is being sucked out of me. Billy Corgan's voice is a salve.

Pushing Cleo into her hands, I say, "Mattie? You're going to get through this. I promise." Then I climb into bed and wrap my arms around her, pretending we're stranded in Antarctica and I have to use my body heat to keep her alive. Strangely, it's only after I hug her that she starts shivering.

The lack of sleep is catching up with me. I drink cup after cup of coffee, but it does nothing to stop my drooping eyelids. I try to stay on my feet and be productive. I check on Mattie every half hour. At lunchtime, I bring her a sandwich and some yogurt. She just leaves the food on her bedside table, untouched.

After forcing myself to nibble on a sandwich of my own, I retreat to the bathroom. I am fading. I fill a glass with water and use it to wash down some caffeine pills, but I am not quick enough. Too late, I realize I'm holding the Scooby-Doo glass that Officer Teahen used the day he visited our house.

Too late, I realize he must have imprinted on the glass.

Too late, I realize I'm going to slide.

I fall to the bathroom floor in a heap.

Officer Teahen is sweating. His shirt is damp with moisture. When he was at our house that day, he seemed so calm and collected as he questioned Mattie. But now, I realize his heart is pounding. He does a great job of hiding his feelings.

He's in a bare room with cement walls, furnished with only a table and two folding chairs. Hanging from the ceiling, a fluorescent light illuminates every corner.

A mirror stretches almost the entire length of one wall, and I've seen enough cop shows to know this is a two-way mirror. Seated at the table, looking extremely ill, is Mr. Golden.

Officer Teahen takes out the same little notepad he used when he questioned Mattie and retrieves a pencil from his pocket. "Tell me again, *why* were you at the high school last night?" He turns around to face Mr. Golden.

"I wasn't feeling well, so I was preparing my lesson plans for the substitute teacher." Beads of sweat materialize on Mr. Golden's forehead.

"What time was this?"

"Um, about nine forty-five."

Officer Teahen makes a note of the time. "Tell me what happened then. Don't leave anything out."

Mr. Golden takes a deep breath. "Well, I waved to Eddie—the night custodian—and went to my classroom. I wrote my lesson plans on the board and set out some work sheets on my desk. Then I left."

"How long did this take?" Officer Teahen taps his pencil against the notepad thoughtfully.

"Fifteen minutes. Maybe twenty."

"And that's when you heard the shot?"

Mr. Golden squeezes his eyes shut. "Yes. About ten fifteen."

"And what did you do then?"

Mr. Golden opens his eyes. "I went out to the football field, where I heard the shot. And I found—I called 911 right away."

Officer Teahen takes a minute to ask the next question. I get the sense he's struggling with how to phrase it. Finally, he asks, "Mr. Golden, what was your relationship with Amber Prescott?"

Mr. Golden looks dazed. "She was in my sixth-period class."

"Nothing beyond that? You never spoke with her outside of school?"

"No." Mr. Golden sounds agitated.

"What about Sophie Jacobs? What was your relationship with her?"

"She was in my eighth period."

"Some students have stated that they saw you driving with her in your vehicle. Is that true?"

Mr. Golden shrugs nervously. "I gave her a ride home sometimes."

"That was it?"

Mr. Golden pauses, and Officer Teahen rushes on. "Mr. Golden, were you aware that Sophie Jacobs was pregnant?"

Mr. Golden bows his head. After a long, long moment, he whispers, "Yes."

Mattie's scream brings me back. The noise is multilayered, peal upon peal of shock and terror. I am crumpled on the bathroom floor.

"Mattie, stop. It's okay. I'm okay." I crawl toward her and pull myself to my feet. As she nestles her head into the crook of my neck, her screams subside.

I hear the front door open.

"Girls?" my father calls. Mattie breaks away from me and races toward the sound of his voice. I follow her down the stairs and watch them embrace. He squeezes her tight, and it makes me wish I could feel the warmth of him.

"Are you girls okay?" It's a dumb question. He turns a little pink.

The officer's conversation with Mr. Golden hangs somewhere in the back of my head. I need to get away, go someplace to sort out my thoughts.

"I'm going out," I announce, grabbing my jacket from the coatrack.

"Where are you going?" my father demands, grabbing my wrist, sounding panicked. I know he's afraid to be alone with Mattie and her grief, but I need a break. I shake him off.

"For a walk. I'll be back soon."

With that, I slip out the door.

I walk quickly to keep warm. It seems the temperature is dipping lower every day now. Before long, the dead leaves will be covered with snow. Pure, white snow. That thought cheers me a little.

In my head, I replay the scene at the police station. It seems clear that Officer Teahen believes Golden is involved with the girls' deaths somehow. He seemed to be insinuating that the teacher was having an inappropriate relationship with Sophie or Amber or both of them. If you'd asked me a few weeks ago whether Golden was capable of such a thing, I'd have said hell no. He was a cool teacher. Everyone liked him. But I guess appearances can be deceiving.

I turn onto the next street, Arbor. At the very end is a light-blue house with a picket fence. Until recently, a slanted For Sale sign had been stuck in the front yard. This is the house Zane was talking about. This is where he lives.

Without thinking, I climb the porch and gently rap on the door with my knuckles. A moment passes, and I hear voices somewhere in the house. Someone tromps on the stairs.

Zane flings open the door and looks at me in surprise. "Vee. What are you doing here? Is everything okay?"

"Yes. No. I'm just . . . I need a jelly doughnut."

Zane's eyebrows knit together. "I don't have any left. I'm sorry." His earnestness makes me smile, in spite of myself.

"Oh, no. Metaphorical jelly doughnuts, you know? I need to talk."

"Ah," he says. "Metaphorical jelly doughnuts I can do. You want to sit down?" He motions toward a couple of rocking chairs. I ease into one and survey the street. The neighborhood I've lived in my whole life seems different somehow, from this angle.

"What's up?"

A sob bubbles up in my throat. I clamp my hands over my mouth, a little embarrassed at the sound. I've only known this boy for a few days. I'm really starting to like him. Do I want to bawl like a baby in front of him?

Zane sits in the chair next to me and pries away one of my hands. He holds it in his own, soft and hard at the same time. He slides his finger back and forth over the skin between my thumb and pointer finger. It makes me shiver.

"Someone else died," I say. "Another of my sister's friends."

He leans forward, concerned. I tell him about my father's phone call and how I spent the whole day watching over Mattie.

I tell him I'm scared. So scared.

I'm scared my sister won't make it through this alive.

Through it all, he keeps rubbing my hand, and it's his touch that gives me the courage to keep going. When I finish, we just sit there. Across the street, a girl in a purple cape chases a small, yapping dog. Oh, what I wouldn't give to be that girl.

I fold myself into the space between his arm and his body. I let myself melt into him, and I can feel him pressing back into me.

"Zane?"

"Yeah?"

"You told me about a sister. What happened?"

He draws a breath, then lets it out slowly. "She died in the hospital shortly after she was born. I don't know what exactly was wrong with her. My mom doesn't like to talk about it."

His eyes dim as he speaks. I think about all the pain he's gone through in his life—his father's suicide, his sister's death. I wonder if some of us are just destined to know tragedy personally. We are alike that way.

"That must have been so hard."

"I don't remember much about her. I worry about my mom, though. Ever since we've been back, it's like the past has started to haunt her. She walks around in a sort of haze. I try to get her to go out, do things, meet people. But she won't. She's . . . fixated."

His worry about his mother touches me. I wrap my arms around him, tight. He nuzzles his nose into the hollow of my neck, and then follows with his lips.

As he kisses me, I feel like the lies and death and evil that surround me slowly melt away, and I am new again.

CHAPTER NINETEEN

I look in on Mattie before I leave for school. She doesn't stir. She sleeps the dreamless sleep of Ambien, but that's a good thing. Without it, I don't know what she'd dream of. Dying cheerleaders, broken bodies. She's better off blank. For a moment, I pause, wondering if I shouldn't stay home to watch over her, but I figure she'll be safe with my dad.

In the driveway, Zane waits. I buckle my seat belt, though it won't do anything to protect me from the wreck that awaits us at school. The principal has dismissed regular classes for the day and arranged an assembly.

When we arrive at school, we have to park across the street because the football field and most of the parking lot are blocked off with yellow police tape.

A couple of kids from Wise Choices usher everyone into the gym. They wear T-shirts that say FEELING BLUE? TELL SOMEONE. The bleachers are packed with antsy students and a few concerned-looking parents. I stand at the bottom for a moment, eyeing the stands. Rollins is nowhere to be seen. Neither is Scotch, for that matter.

The air buzzes with rumors. Everyone has their own theory about what happened to Amber. Some kids whisper that she was jealous of Sophie's affair with Mr. Golden. Others say she killed herself out of guilt for pushing Sophie to the edge. Everyone knows how she sent that naked picture of Sophie to the entire football team.

I want to scream my suspicions out loud. *Sophie didn't kill herself. Amber didn't kill herself. There is a murderer among us, and everyone better watch out.* Instead, I concentrate on putting one foot in front of the other as Zane and I climb the bleachers. We find seats in the back, overlooking the entire student body and the nervous, shuffling teachers.

Zane squeezes my hand. "Everything is going to be okay." Even though I'm sure he's wrong, I appreciate the effort.

Three gigantic screens are set up on the gym floor. The middle one is parallel with the bleachers, and the other two are angled inward. Suddenly, the lights go out, and a projector begins flashing images and words onto the screens to the beat of a loud rock song. The pictures are of attractive, yet depressed, teenagers. A redhead fights with her friends. A guy in a baseball cap mopes on the steps in front of his school, his head in his hands. A beautiful blonde stands in front of a mirror, contemplating a bottle of pills.

Words like *sadness*, *loneliness*, and *depression* are interspersed with the pictures. The show goes on for about five minutes, and then one last slide pops up, stretching across all three screens. It's the number for a suicide hotline.

"I think I'm going to be sick," I mutter.

It's gotten so hot. I can't breathe. I Need. To. Get. Out. Of. Here.

Releasing Zane's hand, I rise to go. He stands, as if to come with me, but I push him away. I just want to be alone. I just need the space to breathe. Somehow, I manage to pick my way down the bleachers and slip out of the gym.

The air in the hallway is much cooler. I lean against a trophy case filled with polished gold footballs and basketballs and squeeze my eyes shut, trying to figure out what bothered me so much about the assembly—beyond the obvious fact that it was arranged under completely false assumptions.

I think, though, that I still would have been sickened, even if Sophie and Amber really had committed suicide. There was something so commercial about it, something contrived. It was like the slide show was designed by MTV. I'm on *True Life: Someone Is Killing All the Cheerleaders and Making It Look Like Suicide.*

When the vomity feeling passes, I wander away from the display case, down the hall, toward the girls' bathroom. I round a corner and stop dead in my tracks.

Halfway down the hall, Scotch is shuffling some papers inside a locker.

I take a step backward, out of sight. What would Scotch be doing in the freshman hallway? After a few seconds, I hear a locker door slam. I tense up when I hear his footsteps, but they get softer and softer. He's going the other way.

Cautiously, I poke my head out to see if he's gone. I

glimpse the back of his jacket as he turns a corner and heads toward the student exit. Something black is crumpled on the floor about halfway down the hallway.

I count to ten, in case Scotch realizes he dropped something and comes back for it. When he doesn't, I come out from my hiding spot and make my way toward the black thing. It's a leather glove.

A thought flashes through my mind: *Maybe I can use this.*

I don't know why I didn't think of it before. I've always thought of my sliding as a disability, something that happened *to* me without my consent. But what if I could somehow force myself to slide while holding that glove?

The idea of entering Scotch's head chills me. Every time I see him, I feel physically ill. I was barely able to handle my encounter with him when I slid into Amber. Would I really be capable of purposefully sliding into him?

I picture my sister—at home, in bed, in an Ambien coma. Helpless. If I don't do something to figure out who the killer is, she could very well be next.

I make my decision. I swoop down, pick up the glove, and stuff it into my pocket. Once it's there, I get a little paranoid that Scotch will realize he dropped his glove and come back, so I backtrack toward the gym.

All the classrooms are dark and empty, except for one—Mr. Golden's room. When I passed by it before, I hadn't noticed the light on, but now I realize someone is inside. I approach it cautiously and stand just outside the door, peeking in. Principal Nast is standing with his back to me, and Mr. Golden is sitting at his desk, looking down at his folded hands. I step back slightly so that he won't see me if he looks up.

Mr. Nast speaks first, sounding kind of embarrassed. "Joe, is it true that you knew about Sophie Jacobs's pregnancy?"

A pause.

"Yes. She came in on Friday to talk to me about the situation."

Nast clears his throat. "Can you tell me who the father is?"

"I'm sorry, Steve, but I just don't feel comfortable giving you that information. The girl is dead. Shouldn't she have some privacy?"

"Here's the thing. I've been getting some complaints. All these rumors are making parents nervous about you teaching their kids. Any information you gave me at this point would help me to clear your name. Otherwise, I'm going to need you to take a leave of absence until this thing blows over."

Another pause.

"Joe, I'm trying to help you here."

Mr. Golden says nothing.

Mr. Nast makes a frustrated sound and exits the room. As he passes by me, I turn to a random locker and spin the lock. He glares at me before heading toward the gym. When he's gone, I peer into Mr. Golden's room. He hasn't moved. He's just sitting there, staring at his hands.

The new, proactive me whispers that I should try to get some information from him. Even if he is the killer, there's not much he can do to me here at school. Maybe I can even sneak something with his imprint on it, something that will help me check up on him later.

"Mr. Golden?" I take a step inside. He raises his head, looking confused at the sound of his own name. "Hey . . . uh, I had some questions about the reading assignment. Do you have a minute?"

He stares at me like I'm from another planet.

"Mr. Golden? Are you okay?"

He heaves an enormous sigh. "I can't believe this is my life." He seems to be talking to himself more than to me. He goes to the closet, pulls out a box, and returns to his desk. He starts throwing random things inside—a half-empty bag of cough drops, a stuffed Homer Simpson doll, some *Newsweek* magazines.

"People have been talking. They think I had something to do with the deaths." He forms his syllables in a simple monotone—no inflection whatsoever. He doesn't sound angry or upset or anything. Just numb.

"Why would they think that?" I ask carefully.

"Because people want someone to blame," Mr. Golden replies bitterly. "Sophie came to me for help. I go to her church, and I know her family. When she got pregnant, she asked me for advice. I guess someone saw us together and got the wrong idea."

I think carefully about his words. Would a teacher drive a student around, even if they were a friend of the family? Even if they did go to church together? It still seems suspicious.

"Now that Amber's dead, people are making up all

kinds of stories. I tell you, people just want to believe the worst." He mutters something about a "goddamn witch hunt" and then goes back to packing up his things.

"So what are you going to do?" I ask, looking around his room for something that would fit in my pocket.

"What *can* I do? I'm going to go home."

I hear voices in the hallway. The assembly must be over.

"I should leave," I say.

"You probably should," Mr. Golden says, turning back to his desk.

That's when I see it—sitting right there, in plain sight. It was there all the time. Why didn't I notice it before?

The desk calendar.

It looks so harmless—just a plain desk calendar that you'd pick up at any office supply store. White pages, with the month and date in a thick, black font. Just like the page that was stuck to my front door the day Sophie died.

I feel like I can't breathe. My heart is hammering underneath my shirt. Somehow, I force myself to turn around naturally and head for the door. I look back once, to make sure Mr. Golden is still focused on packing, and then I dart my hand out and grab a tiny figurine from the bookshelf next to the door.

And then I'm gone.

I feel my phone vibrate in my pocket as I tread my way through the sea of students.

"Hello?"

It's my father. "Hey, Vee—could you do me a favor and

pick up Mattie's books? I have a feeling she'll be missing at least a few more days. It'd be nice if she could make up some schoolwork at home."

"Uh, sure," I say, and then hang up. When I put my phone away, I pull the stolen figurine out of my pocket. It's a tiny bronze statue of Sigmund Freud. It seems like the sort of thing Mr. Golden would cherish. Sticking it back in my pocket, I hope he's left some sort of emotional charge on the object. I really don't want to return to his room to try to get something else.

Students rush past me, heading for the exit. They chat excitedly, thrilled to get an early start on the weekend. I fight my way toward my sister's locker. A well-placed punch causes it to pop right open.

I gasp.

Everything in her locker has been tossed to the floor—her textbooks, her gym clothes, the pictures of her and Sophie and Amber that had been taped to the inside of the door. All of it is jumbled at the bottom of her locker.

Kneeling, I pick up a piece of a photograph that's been ripped to pieces. Half of my sister's face, painted to look like a cat, smiles.

I try to drop the picture, but it clings to my fingers. It's covered with a sticky, red substance. When I realize what it is, my stomach drops, and I cover my mouth, afraid I'm going to vomit.

The bottom of Mattie's locker is covered in blood.

I open my mouth and scream.

"What's wrong? Vee?" Strong hands grasp my shoulders.

I turn around, see that it's Zane, and bury my head against his chest.

We're sitting in Zane's car, waiting for the parking lot to clear out. He traces circles on my back with his fingertip as I wait for my dad to pick up the phone.

"Pick up, pick up, pick up."

"Hello?"

"Dad," I say. "Um, I tried to get Mattie's books, but I couldn't remember her combination. Could you ask her for me?" I don't want to tell my father the bottom of Mattie's locker was coated with red paint. I need to figure out what it means first. I just need him to tell me that Mattie's okay.

I listen to him shuffle around, praying that he'll find Mattie safe in her bed. I hear muffled voices, and I let out a sigh of relief. If the mess in Mattie's locker was meant to be a warning, the killer hasn't struck yet.

"She says nineteen, thirty-four, eighty-six," my dad says. "Thanks for doing this."

"No problem," I say, looking at the pile of books stashed by my feet. I tried to clean them off the best I could, but they're still pretty gross. I'll have to figure out how to explain that later, I guess. "I'll be home soon."

I hang up and sit motionless, staring at my phone.

"When is this going to end?" I wonder aloud.

"When is what going to end?" Zane asks.

"This insanity. When is it going to end? Sophie's dead. Amber's dead. And now someone is targeting my sister." It occurs to me that Scotch was in the hall minutes before me. If he wasn't at the assembly, what was he doing?

"Do you really think someone wants to hurt Mattie?" he asks.

"Why else would someone do that to her locker? It's a pretty sick prank to play on someone right after two of her friends die. God. It looked so much like blood," I say, remembering the way Sophie's white sheets had turned all scarlet and clotty, just like the stuff at the bottom of Mattie's locker. My hands haven't stopped shaking.

"I'm so worried about Mattie," I continue. "She's depressed. Her two best friends are gone. What if . . . What if she tries to . . . ?"

Zane puts a finger to my lips. "It'll be okay. We'll stay with her this weekend. Watch movies. Make sure she doesn't even leave the house."

He's right, I think. *I'll keep her safe by getting to the bottom of all this. I'll figure out how to make myself slide and find out who the killer is. And, somehow, I will make them pay.*

"Vee?" Zane says.

"Yes?" I reply, my mind somewhere else—on sliding and killers and blood. But when he leans in and kisses me, he has my full attention.

He whispers, "I think I'm falling for you."

For some reason, I can't make my mouth work; I can't voice the words that are carved into my heart. Instead of speaking, I wrap my arms around him and hold tight.

CHAPTER TWENTY

itting on my bed, I clamp my hand over my mouth and stifle a yawn. I haven't had any caffeine in approximately nine hours—since before I left for school. Bad things happen to me when I don't get my caffeine. Headache, major grouchiness, nausea.

It'll all be worth it if I can find out what happened to Sophie and Amber before the killer strikes again, I think as I rub my temples.

When my eyelids feel like lead weights, I decide it is time. I hold Scotch's glove in my bare hands. I rub the material, the coarseness making my skin crawl.

I wait.

Nothing happens.

I wait some more.

Nothing.

This isn't as easy as I thought it would be, I think, slapping the glove against my thigh. I suppose it's possible Scotch never imprinted on the glove. He doesn't seem like the most emotional person in the world.

What will I do if it doesn't work? I picture myself sneaking into Scotch's house late at night and grabbing something I know he cares about. Something like a football or a girlie magazine. I'm just fooling myself, though. It would be stupid to break into a possible killer's house. This *has* to work.

Beside me, my phone rings. Rollins again. He's been calling all afternoon. Each time, I let it go to voice mail. At first, he left messages for me to call him back. Now he just hangs up when I don't answer.

It's not that I don't want to talk to him. I do. I want him to explain exactly what he was doing with Amber on that field moments before her death. The thing is, I can't ask him that question. I can't explain how I know he was there. And until I know for sure who killed Sophie, I can't risk letting him get close to me—and more importantly, to Mattie.

The phone goes silent.

Good.

I return to my task. Rubbing the glove against my cheek, I inhale the scent of Scotch. Of sweat, of orange shampoo. Of that night so long ago. My stomach turns over.

The seconds slip by. Soon I start to feel sleepy.

The room goes dark, and I lose my grip on the present. I slide.

A dark room materializes around me, lit only by a football game on the television. Faux wood paneling stretches from one wall to the next. There are several framed posters featuring football players I don't recognize. I'm lounging in a leather chair, a can of something cold in my hand. Scotch lifts the drink and takes a sip. Expecting something sweet, I'm surprised at the bitter taste that fills my mouth.

Beer.

What is Scotch doing drinking beer in the middle of the afternoon?

He opens his mouth, and a deep voice—much deeper than Scotch's—calls out, "Tricia? Trish! I thought I told you to make me a damn sandwich."

A petite woman enters my line of vision, holding another beer in one hand and a plate in the other.

"Sorry, Hank. I was just finishing up some laundry."

Hank.

Not Scotch.

I've slid into his father.

Damn.

I wake up on my bed, pillow cushioning my head.

Someone thumps on my door and then opens it without waiting for an answer.

"Vee?" My father looks in. "Did you bring home Mattie's books?"

"Um, yeah," I say, sitting up. I point to a pile of books sitting on my mother's rocking chair. "Unfortunately, I set them down in the hall while I went to the bathroom, and the custodian was walking by with a can of paint. And he tripped. . . ."

I look at my father's face to gauge whether he's buying any of this at all. He drifts into the room, nodding distractedly. I don't think he's even paying attention.

"So that assembly you went to today—was it helpful? They talked to you about the warning signs of suicide, right?" My father ruffles his hands through his hair.

"Right," I say, even though I didn't sit through the whole thing.

He sits down heavily on my bed. "Did Sophie or Amber exhibit any of those signs?"

His question catches me off guard. I try to remember the warning signs. I know the counselors told us all about them when we were in middle school. The only one I recall is giving away personal belongings. I shiver when I remember Sophie giving me the bracelet to give to Mattie. But that was a gift. . . . It doesn't count, does it?

"I don't know. They weren't exactly *my* friends."

"I think I'm going to call Dr. Moran. Mattie should have someone to talk to. Someone who knows about these things."

Hearing the name of my old psychiatrist irritates me. She's the cold, unsympathetic woman my father sent me to when he thought I was lying about sliding. The one who accused me of making up stories for attention. I know Mattie probably needs professional help, but I hate the thought of sending her to that robot.

"Whatever," I mutter, but my father has already risen and is crossing to the door.

For once, I wish he'd realize that what Mattie needs is *him*.

After dinner, I have an idea. A breakthrough.

I fling open my closet door and stand there for a moment, my heart pounding. Then I push my clothes aside until I come to the one garment I know Scotch had his hands on—the purple dress I wore to homecoming.

My hands shaking, I carry the dress over to my bed and carefully spread it out. I smooth my hands over it. The fabric sparkles as it moves. As I stare at the dress, I'm filled with certainty that this will work. The dress will put me in Scotch's head. I've been going about it all wrong. Clearly, Scotch never imprinted on the glove. But this dress—I know he felt something strong when he touched this dress.

I kneel at the side of my bed and rest my hands lightly on the material. And, just as I knew it would, the room fades away.

Tombstones. Everywhere.

Scotch is in the cemetery. The sun has sunk low in the sky. It also seems several degrees colder than it did when I was outside, but then I realize it must be because Scotch only has one glove. He raises his bare hand to his mouth and blows into it, the hot air warming it only slightly.

A huge, gnarled tree looms over us. When Scotch passes it, I see a woman in a red coat stooped in front of a tiny gravestone, clutching a fistful of daisies. She kneels down and brushes away some leaves, and I'm able to read the inscription.

Sadness squeezes my heart. The baby died after only two days of life. If the child had lived, she'd be in my sister's grade.

The woman at the grave turns toward Scotch and brushes her white hair out of her face. Her eyes are black as coal and filled with sadness, and I wonder what losing a child that young does to you. I'm reminded of the passage on black holes in my astronomy book, how they suck everything in until no light remains. That's what seeing your kid die must feel like.

Scotch seems to feel the pull of her misery, too, but he looks away and continues walking. We pass by the nine-foot statue of an angel that used to be bronze. Years of harsh weather have turned it black. Rumor has it, if you kiss the angel, you will drop dead within one year.

Scotch keeps going until he comes to a delicate, white, brand-new tombstone.

SOPHIE JACOBS

Scotch just stands there, staring at the piece of stone that marks the grave of a girl who might have carried his child. Again, I wish I could know his thoughts. Why would he come here? To gloat that he got away with murder? To make amends? To mourn?

He reaches out his naked hand and traces Sophie's name with his fingers. "I wish it could have been different, Soph.

I really do." He retrieves his hand and pushes it into his pocket. "I guess God just didn't want me to get tied down this early in life. It's probably for the best."

A terrible rage rises within me. The fury is energy, begging to be used. Gathering all my strength, I form Scotch's hand into a fist and slam it into his balls. The pain is beyond belief, but I know it's so much worse for him.

He screams, and it's the last thing I hear as I'm pulled away from his body.

CHAPTER TWENTY-ONE

I toss and turn, trying to turn my mind off, trying to will myself to fall asleep, but I'm not tired at all. Actually, I've never felt so alive, so energized. When I guided Scotch's muscles, it was like I was inside him, only not. It was like a video game, like I was pushing buttons with my mind, and he did what I told him. It was invigorating.

For so long, I've been out of control, popping in and out of people's heads, prisoner to their choices and actions. Now there is a sliver of light, of hope, that I can *choose*.

If I slide into a teacher making out with a bus driver during school hours, I can choose to push him and his disgusting mustache away.

If I slide into Scotch when he's putting his hands all over some clueless cheerleader, I can *choose* to neuter him. Oh, and don't think I won't.

If I slide into someone standing in a dark room and there's the smell of blood and I see a body on the bed, I can . . .

I can . . .

I can't do anything about that.

I can't do anything about Sophie.

And I can't do anything about Amber, either.

But *now.* Now that I have some control, maybe I can keep other girls from dying. Maybe I can protect my sister.

I jump onto my bed and start doing ninja kicks and punching the air. I am Buffy, ready to kick some bad-guy ass. Laughter erupts from my throat, and I flop down onto my bed and stare at the planet and star stickers on my ceiling.

This feeling of being in charge of my own life is intoxicating. I feel drunk or high or something. I want to use my new power, want to experiment.

I slip out of my bedroom and tiptoe down the hall. I peer down the stairs and see light coming from my father's office. He's probably busy with his online forum, comforting cancer survivors, saying just the right things to them because he doesn't have to sit across from them at dinner.

I continue down the hall, to his bedroom. The door is slightly ajar. I push it the rest of the way open and look around. His room is perfectly neat. The bed is made, and—unlike my room—there are no clothes on the floor. There's nothing on top of the chest of drawers except an old picture of my mother.

My father keeps his and my mother's wedding rings in a velvet box in the top right drawer of the bureau. For years after her death, he kept wearing his ring, until an old lady on the cancer survivors' forum told him he should take it off. For once, he took someone else's advice instead of dishing it out. When I noticed he wasn't wearing it anymore, I asked him about it. He assured me he was keeping it safe, but it was painful to keep looking down at his hand and missing Mom all day long. Sometimes I go into the drawer and open the box—not to touch the rings, but just to look at them. This time, I carefully pull my father's ring out of the box.

I've slid into my father before—accidentally, when I tried on his watch or flipped through an old photo album. Once I slid into him in the middle of an operation, and that pretty much scarred me for life. But since I know he's downstairs right now, messing around on the computer, I figure he's the perfect target for my little test.

Back in my room, I hop onto my bed and cup the ring in my palm.

I sit there for a long time, waiting for something— anything—to happen. The minutes pass by slowly. After a while, I start to get paranoid that my father will come upstairs and look in his drawer. There's no reason for him to, but I guess that's the nature of paranoia.

I slip the ring onto my finger and lie back on my pillow. My headache from earlier returns, and it seems like the caffeine pills in my backpack are actually calling out to me, begging me to swallow a few of them. Ignoring the pain, I close my eyes.

And feel myself go.

I find myself in my father's office, sitting before his computer. He's reading an email from some lady who lost her son to cancer last year. For a moment he stares at the screen, probably thinking of how to phrase his response.

Then he hits Reply and types a few sentences expressing his condolences and recommending a book that will help her manage her grief.

After sending that email, he minimizes the page with the cancer survivor forum and pulls up an online medical journal. He clicks through a couple of articles, reading about recent surgeries. It's pretty boring. I wonder if I should make him pick his nose or something, just to see if I can do it.

I concentrate all my energy into his right pointer finger. *Come on, finger*, I think. *Pick Dad's nose*. But the finger just keeps floating around the trackpad on my dad's computer, navigating him through article after boring article.

Frustrated, I try to figure out why I can't control my father like I controlled Scotch in the cemetery. The only thing I can come up with is the rage I felt when Scotch said he thought Sophie's death was for the best. Maybe adrenaline has something to do with it.

The phone rings, and my dad jumps a little. He brings the phone to his ear and says hello, but all I hear is heavy breathing.

"Hello? Hello?" my father repeats, annoyance edging his voice. No one replies. "Goddamn it, this is the last straw. If you call here again, I'm going to call the police." Whoever is on the other end hangs up the phone.

I wonder who it was. I'm filled with apprehension as I remember the phone call I overheard the other day when he was telling someone it was over. Could my father have a stalker?

He sits quietly for a second before hanging up, staring at

the wedding picture of my mother. He takes it in his hands.

I expect him to caress my mother's image or kiss it or something, but instead he flips it over and unhooks the back. To my surprise, he reveals a tiny silver key taped to the underside of the photograph. Carefully, he unpeels the tape and takes the key into his hand. Then he reassembles the frame and returns the picture to his desk.

I watch in astonishment as he takes the little key and guides it into the lock on the bottom drawer of the desk.

My parents bought the desk from a flea market ages ago. When we were little, my sister and I used it to play teacher. We tried to pull the drawer open, but it never budged. Dad said the previous owner of the desk had lost the key, but it was so beautiful he just had to have it anyway.

He lied.

He pulls the drawer open and shoves his hand inside, searching roughly for something. Finally he pulls out a manila folder. Across the front, written in my father's messy handwriting, is the name Allison. He flips it open, revealing a thick sheaf of papers. On the very top is a photograph of a gorgeous woman with white-blond hair.

The realization is sudden—I have seen that woman before. In the cemetery, when I slid into Scotch. She was standing before a tombstone. A tombstone marked ALLISON MORROW. Trying to piece it all together, I wonder who exactly that woman is. And who the hell is Allison?

My father's hands shake as he puts the folder back in the drawer, minus the picture of the white-haired woman. He stares at the picture for a moment longer, before crinkling it up in his fist. He tosses the picture into the wastebasket beneath his desk.

"Leave. Me. Alone," he whispers.

He then locks the drawer and puts the key back in its hiding place.

Slowly, I feel myself being pulled away, back into my own body.

After I hear my father go into his room, I wait half an hour and then open my door silently. Down the hall, my father's room is quiet, no light peeking beneath the door. I pray that he's asleep. I tiptoe down the stairs, the cold wood freezing my bare feet.

My father's office is dark, lit only by the moonlight coming through the window. It really is a dreary place, now that I think about it. When my mother was alive, she decorated every room to her taste, bringing in paintings and floral prints and pretty mirrors. But my dad never let her touch this room. He doesn't even let Vanessa clean in here. There's a layer of sludge on the windows. This room is full of his things, his dusty secrets.

I dash across the room and snatch up the picture of my mother. Removing the back of the frame, I find the key just where my father left it, shining so brightly it seems as though it's daring me to use it.

I stare at it for a moment. What will it lead me to? I don't know. I'm not sure I'm ready to know, but I don't know if I'll ever really be ready, so I carefully peel away the tape and weigh the key in the palm of my hand. So light, yet so heavy at the same time.

Kneeling down, I position the key by the lock. For a split second, I chicken out. This is my dad, the guy who cooks us chocolate-chip pancakes every Sunday morning. He has to have a good reason for keeping whatever it is locked up in there.

Doesn't he?

My eyes flicker involuntarily to the trash can, willing the picture of the white-haired woman to be gone. Maybe it was all in my head. All my imagination. But there it still is.

I'm tired of secrets.

I'm ready for truth.

I force the key into the lock and twist until I hear a little click release somewhere inside the wooden desk. I set the key on top of the desk and pull open the drawer. The manila folder sits on top of a bunch of old medical journals. I snatch the folder up and riffle through the papers within. They're some kind of records.

I pull out a paper and examine it.

Name: Allison Annette Morrow

Allison Morrow. The name from the tombstone. The girl who died after only a couple of days. Why would my father be keeping her medical records?

I continue reading. There's a bunch of gibberish I don't understand. She was born prematurely with an anorectal malformation and required immediate surgery. I flip a page. Numbers. Jargon.

I turn to the last page in the folder.

Date of death: October 19, 1998

October 19. Allison Annette Morrow died in surgery just over fourteen years ago under my father's knife. And he keeps her medical records in a drawer, never to forget. I feel sick.

Why her?

I know he's lost babies before.

Why hold on to this one failure?

My hands shaking, I replace the folder on top of the magazines. I lock the drawer and return the key to its hiding place.

It takes me a long, long time to fall asleep.

CHAPTER TWENTY-TWO

Today is Mattie's birthday, and I haven't gotten her a thing.

I only remember when I see the special breakfast casserole on the kitchen table—the one my father reserves for birthdays or other special occasions. Eggs and bacon and cheese and potatoes. And butter. Lots and lots of butter. Normally, I live for this sort of thing, but these words keep sliding around my head: *anorectal malformation*. I Googled the term last night, but knowing the medical details didn't help much. I want to know exactly what happened on October 19, 1998, and why my father has held on to it for so long. What's so special about this Allison? And what's his connection with the white-haired woman I saw in the cemetery?

I don't know how to broach this topic. Plus, Mattie has actually brushed her hair and is sitting at the table, looking hungry, so I don't want to do anything to mess that up.

"So, what do you want to do for your big day, birthday girl?" My dad heaps a pile of casserole onto a plate and passes it to Mattie. The forced cheeriness in his voice seems to highlight how crappy this day actually is.

Mattie shrugs and then pushes a fork into the melty, cheesy mess in front of her. "I don't know. Just hang out around here? I don't really feel like going out."

"That sounds great. Maybe we could rent *Mulan* tonight? Order pizza for dinner? Would you like that?"

"Dad, I haven't liked *Mulan* since the second grade," Mattie replies. There's no resentment in her voice, like there would have been had I said it. It's just a simple fact.

"Well, how about the first season of *Rumor Girl*? I've heard great things." My father's face is so earnest, it's almost painful to look at.

"Um, you mean *Gossip Girl*? Sure. Yeah, okay." My sister takes another glob of casserole into her mouth.

Could my father really be hiding some deep, dark secret? This man who wants to watch *Gossip Girl* with his teenage daughters? Is this just a facade so we won't suspect what he's *really* up to?

"I'm not feeling well," I say. "I'm going to go lie down."

Passing by my sister, I squeeze her shoulder. "Happy birthday, Matt."

She turns her head my way and gives me the most heart-breaking smile. "Thanks."

Guilt follows me up the stairs and into my room. I really should give her something to acknowledge her birthday—but what?

I scan my belongings, wondering if there's anything I have that she could possibly want. My closet door is ajar, and the box of my mother's CDs is sticking out slightly.

With a tug, I heave the box into the middle of the room.

One by one, I pull the CDs out and spread them all over the floor. Pearl Jam. The Smashing Pumpkins. Veruca Salt. Nirvana. Liz Phair. Ani DiFranco. This is what I have left of my mother, the music she lived her life by.

This is what I have to give to my sister, who was so little when my mother died, who can no longer remember that my mother's hair always smelled like violets or how the corners of her eyes crinkled when she smiled.

I pick up the Smashing Pumpkins CD and hold it to my cheek. The plastic is cold from sitting in my drafty closet for so long. Then I put it back in the box. I go through this process with each CD, holding it close for just one more moment and then putting it away.

When I've loaded the CDs all back into the box, I push the flaps closed and carry it to my sister's room. She hasn't returned from breakfast yet, so I place the box on her unmade bed and leave the room.

I've attached a pink Post-it note. It says:

This is who she was.

Love, V

CHAPTER TWENTY-THREE

I lean back against my pillow, holding the tiny Sigmund Freud and wondering if it is personal enough to provide me with a link to Mr. Golden. It seems like the sort of thing someone would give you for a present. Maybe a family member? A former student? A girlfriend? I rub my thumb over the figure, thinking about what he might have witnessed in Mr. Golden's room.

I turn the little man over. That's when I notice the markings on the bottom. It's been engraved. The letters are so tiny, I have to squint to make out the message.

YOU HYPNOTIZE ME. N.P.

Hmmmm. N.P. Who could that be? Well, one thing's clear—it's a personal item, all right. I just hope he was stirred with enough emotion when he received it to leave an imprint.

When my head starts to pound and black, floaty things swim before my eyes, I know he was. My room disappears, and I am swallowed by the blackness.

Mr. Golden stands before a white door decorated with an orange-and-brown wreath. He balls his right hand into a fist and raps on the door, then takes a step back to wait for an answer. The door opens, revealing a familiar, grief-stricken face. It is Amber Prescott's father. His hair is mussed, and his eyes are rimmed red.

"Mr. Prescott?" Mr. Golden asks, his voice unsure. "I'm Mr. Golden, Amber's teacher. I called earlier. I have the journal she kept in class. Thought you might want it?" He waves a notebook in the air halfheartedly. "Is this a bad time?"

"Uh, no," Amber's father replies, but his voice seems far away, like he's speaking through a fog. "Come in. You can call me Trent."

Mr. Golden steps into the entryway. I survey the scene in agony. I was here once before, briefly, to pick up Mattie from a sleepover. I remember, at the time, being impressed by the simple, elegant decor of the room, from the perfect eggshell paint color to the black suede couch and love seat. The focal point of the room was a painting of purple irises blowing in the wind.

Now, the beautiful painting is askew. Overturned on the coffee table is a single crystal glass in a puddle of brown liquid. The smell assures me that it's something alcoholic. On the muted television, Seinfeld looks like he's laughing.

"Would you care for a drink?"

"Ah, no. Can't stay long. Is your wife around?"

Amber's father eases into a black leather recliner, his eyes glued to the television set. "Back room. She won't come out. Why don't you take the journal to her? It might give her some comfort, to read Amber's words."

Mr. Golden stands there awkwardly for a second, and I'm sure he's considering just tossing the notebook onto the coffee table and getting the hell out of here. That's what I'd be thinking about, anyway. But he surprises me.

He turns and heads down the long hallway, where he must figure the "back room" is. Both walls are lined with pictures. In one, a little Amber stands next to a horse, proudly holding up her blue ribbon. In another, Amber looks to be about ten and sits with her arm hanging casually over her younger brother's shoulder. In yet another, she is older, grinning in a crisp East High cheerleading outfit. She smiles the kind of smile only popular girls own the right to—kind of like, "The world is mine, and that's how it should be." This is the Amber I knew.

The door to the room at the end of the hall is slightly ajar. Mr. Golden holds out his hand and gently pushes it open. For a moment, all I can see is light flickering from votive candles scattered around the floor. Then I realize Amber's mother is sitting in the middle of them, her arms wrapped around her knees. She rocks back and forth, back and forth.

"Nora?" Mr. Golden says, barely above a whisper. Why would he call Amber's father *Mr. Prescott* and her mother *Nora*? The intimacy in the way he said her name is unsettling.

She lifts her head for a moment and then, seeing who it is, lowers it again.

"Nora. I'm here for you." Mr. Golden crouches on the

floor next to her. "I'm here." The tenderness in his voice is palpable. And then it hits me: Nora.

N.P.

Nora Prescott.

Amber's mother must have given him the figurine.

It's as if she doesn't even hear him. She speaks, but it's like she's continuing a different conversation. Her words are barely recognizable, and that's when I smell the liquor on her breath.

"I remember her first day of high school. She said she didn't want to go back. She hated the way everyone pretended to be someone they weren't. She didn't know who to be."

This doesn't sound like the Amber I knew—the girl who plotted which date for homecoming would win her the most popularity, the girl who actually took a ruler to her skirts to see how short she could possibly go without getting busted for breaking the dress code. The Amber I knew was kind of a bitch.

"She was scared, and I made her go back anyway."

The woman takes a sip from a drink I hadn't realized she was holding, then sends it flying through the room. It crashes against the wall and shatters in a burst of ice cubes and jagged pieces of glass.

"I made her *go*."

"She had to go to school, Nora. You most certainly didn't make her steal Trent's gun and do what she did. That was her choice."

Amber's mother turns and looks Mr. Golden in the eyes

for the first time since he entered the room. "She knew about us. The day of Sophie's funeral. She came back just in time to see you leaving. And the next day she shot herself with Trent's gun. Because of us."

My God. The thought that Amber had actually committed suicide never occurred to me. I was sure someone else pulled the trigger, the same someone who dragged the knife across Sophie's wrists. But if Amber used her father's gun, doesn't that mean she killed herself?

"Now, now, Nora. Are you sure she saw me leave? Maybe she was just overcome with sadness. I mean, her best friend had just committed suicide. She was coming home from the funeral." Mr. Golden glances toward the doorway and then reaches over to push Mrs. Prescott's hair out of her face. He sounds calm, reassuring.

What if Amber did come home after Sophie's funeral and ran into Mr. Golden leaving her house? Did she confront him? Did she threaten to tell her father? And if Mr. Golden had access to Mr. Prescott's wife, could he have had access to Mr. Prescott's gun?

Mr. Golden reaches for Mrs. Prescott's hand. She pushes it away and starts mumbling again. He sighs and gets up, leaving the notebook on the floor.

"I'm sorry, Nora," he says, and then exits the room without another word.

CHAPTER TWENTY-FOUR

Luckily, when I return I find my body flopped safely on my bed. I sit up and wipe a bit of drool off my chin. Sliding is not the most glamorous way to get around, that's for sure.

Beside me, my phone rings insistently. Rollins again. My fingers flex, wanting to answer. My gaze falls on the T-shirt he gave me. It lies crumpled on the floor, where I threw it after seeing him with Amber. All I'd have to do is slip it on—I could reassure myself that he had a good reason to meet her that night, that he's not the killer.

I could slide right into his life and find out . . . everything. What he does all those hours he's not at school or work. What he's hiding from me at home. Why he never invites me over. I'm itching to know his secrets, but at the same time I wonder if sliding into him wouldn't be like hacking his email or reading his diary. When I slid into him accidentally, it felt weird, but I knew it wasn't my fault. If I target him by using that same T-shirt, it would be different. It would be like spying.

I'd be doing it for the right reason, though—wouldn't I? To clear Rollins's name. If you invade someone's privacy with good intentions, it's not as bad. I close my eyes and remember how we used to be. I miss our silly conversations about who would win in a fight—Chuck Norris or Mr. T. I miss his sardonic smile. I miss the girl I am when I'm around him.

I have to fix things between us, and sliding into him is the only way I know how.

My decision made, I reach down, snag the blue material with my pinkie, and pull it onto my lap. Easing back onto my pillows, I hug the fabric to my chin. I'm amazed at how quickly I'm taken away. I'm getting kind of good at this.

The smell is acrid, like rotting broccoli and urine. Water stains and cracks work their way down the walls. I'm lying on a mattress with blue flannel sheets, staring up at the ceiling.

A song I know is playing—"Thinking of You" by A Perfect Circle. For a month last year, Rollins was obsessed with this song, playing it on a continuous loop in his car. The drums are intense, beating through my brain.

I'm twirling something in my hands like a baton. Without even looking, I know what it is. A Sharpie. Rollins's sword to tear the world apart. He stops twirling and uses the marker to match the drumbeat on his stomach.

His room is desolate, furnished with only a bed, a small chest of drawers, and a bookcase packed with old paperbacks. Back when we used to hang out, we'd go to the used-book store every weekend and buy bags and bags of books. One of his shelves is dedicated to Stephen King novels. I remember him saying his favorite was *The Dead Zone*.

His door swings open, and a guy in a red flannel shirt bursts in. It must be his uncle Ned.

"You didn't do your shit today," the guy says. It's an accusation—of what, I have no idea.

Rollins sits up. "What shit?"

"It's Saturday. Your turn to do the bath."

Rollins swears. "Can't it wait until tomorrow?"

"She's *your* mother." The man points at Rollins.

Sighing, Rollins stands up and pushes past the man. He walks down the hall and calls to a wiry woman in a wheelchair, who's watching cartoons. Her hair is a tangled nest of snarls.

"Time for your bath," Rollins says, his voice terse.

No wonder he's never invited me to his house. From his surly uncle to his incapacitated mother, he has his hands full without worrying about what his friends think of his predicament. I start to wonder if I made the wrong decision in coming here.

Rollins pushes the woman down the hall and into the bathroom, which looks like it hasn't been cleaned in years. Rollins turns the knob, releasing a gush of water into the tub. He carefully gauges the temperature—not too hot, not too cold.

He helps his mother undress, all the while staring up at the ceiling. She raises her hands, and he pulls off her shirt. She has to lean on him while he lowers her pants and underwear.

I feel that he's turned himself off somehow. He's on autopilot. He helps her into the tub, bearing her weight so she won't slip and fall. He fills a Big Gulp cup and then dumps the water over her head. When he lathers an old pink washcloth with soap and works it over her shoulders and breasts, I zone out.

Before long, the bath is over and Rollins's mother has been toweled off and returned to her place in front of the television. Rollins lumbers back to his room, his fists clenching and unclenching as he passes his uncle, who's cracking open a beer.

As he enters his room, I catch sight of something I'd missed earlier. Peeking out from underneath his bed— which could more accurately be called a cot—is a jumbled pile of photographs.

He walks closer, and in one of the pictures I'm able to make out the shape of a girl in a red bikini lying on a beach towel. Her black hair flares out around her face, and she wears giant red sunglasses. Sophie. What the—?

Apprehension pulses through me. I have to figure out why he has pictures of Sophie. Before I know it, I'm next to the bed and spreading the photographs across the floor.

A part of me realizes that I'm controlling Rollins, but mostly I'm concerned with the task at hand.

There are pictures of Sophie at school, of her in her cheerleading uniform, even in boxers and a T-shirt with her hair twisted into a french braid. Not only that—there are pictures of Amber Prescott, too.

One photograph in particular catches my eye. I grab it so I can examine it more closely. It's a picture of Amber and Sophie at cheerleading practice. In the background, Samantha Phillips stands on top of the bleachers, a megaphone at her mouth. Rollins has drawn devil horns on top of her flaming red hair and a spiky tail curling by her side. In her hand that's not holding the megaphone, he's fashioned a pitchfork.

Why does Rollins have pictures of dead girls in his room?

I set the photo down and stand up, hoping to find a hint somewhere in the room. A closet door beckons to me. When I open it, the contents make me sad. Two pairs of jeans, neatly hung on hangers. And his leather jacket, his most prized possession.

There is literally nothing else in the closet.

Just then, I feel myself start to go.

No, I tell myself. I hold on to Rollins with every fiber of my being. But, as easy as it was for me to slide into him, I'm unable to anchor myself in his body. I stagger backward and leave Rollins lying on his bed.

Hot water cascades over my shoulders and back, pounding out the tension I've felt since coming out of my latest slide. I tilt my head back and let the water run down my face, thinking about what I saw at Rollins's house.

By sliding into Rollins, I'd been hoping to find the reason for his meeting with Amber on the night of her death. But all I turned up were more questions.

On the bright side, I was able to take control of Rollins. I think it has something to do with my focus. When I controlled Scotch, I was so pissed and all I could think about was giving him the beating he so sorely deserved. When I was in Rollins, I was intent on finding out why he had those photographs.

My cell phone, which I set on the edge of the sink in case Zane called while I was showering, begins to ring the generic ring it makes when someone I don't know calls. Squinting, I shut the water off and reach for a towel.

The number flashing on the display looks vaguely familiar, but I can't place it. Iowa City area code, so it's not a telemarketer. I wrap the towel around my torso, tuck the end under my armpit, and pick up the phone.

"Hello?"

"Vee?"

Again, the pang of familiarity strikes, but I can't place the voice that's asking for me.

"Yeah?"

"It's Samantha."

Something like nostalgia hits me, and I wonder if I haven't stepped out of the shower and into last year, when a phone call from Samantha wasn't something unusual. For a minute, I'm speechless, and I just stand there with my mouth open like an idiot.

"Um. Samantha? Why are you calling me? Did you accidentally call the wrong sister? I can go get Mattie for you. It is her birthday, you know. . . ."

"Yeah, well, that's sort of why I'm calling."

"Okay . . . so what do you want?"

"I'm organizing a little get-together at my place tonight. But it's a surprise. I asked her if she wanted to come over and watch movies, but she said she wanted to hang out with family. . . ." The tone of Samantha's voice makes me roll my eyes, like it's so ridiculous Mattie would ever want to spend time with her family.

"Samantha. Two members of your squad are dead. Isn't it a little . . . insensitive to be throwing a party tonight?"

"That's exactly why I'm doing it. I'm guessing Mattie's been just lying around in bed the last couple of days. Am I right? She needs to get out and have some fun. I have her best interests at heart."

"Uh-huh. Well, Mattie can do what she wants. Sorry if that spoils your plans."

Samantha pauses.

"Vee, really. I'm trying to do something nice for Matt. I'm worried about her. With everything that's happened in the past week . . . she needs her friends."

I squelch the snide comment about what kind of a friend I think Samantha is and think of Mattie, shut up in her bedroom like a hermit. It actually would be good for her to get out of the house. Get out of her head. This might not be such a bad idea.

"What do you need me to do?"

"Come to the party. Convince her to go. I'll come and pick you guys up and everything. I know you don't drive. . . ."

Her words trail off, and I know our minds are both back in the gym last year, when she watched Scotch drag my lifeless body into the boys' locker room.

"On one condition," I say.

"Anything," she replies.

"You can't invite Scotch Becker."

"Done."

"Okay. You can pick us up at seven."

My sister's room is dark, with the soft notes of Pearl Jam's "Black" wafting through the air, filling the room with an anguish so thick I think I could touch it. My sister lies on the floor, wrapped in a pink blanket.

"Mattie?"

"Sssssssh, this is the best part," she says, her eyes closed.

So many times I've listened to this song, envisioning a shroud over all the pictures of our dead mother. Samantha is right. I have to dig Mattie out of this hole.

"I love this song," I say, tiptoeing to her computer and finding the pause button. "But don't you think you should listen to something a little more upbeat on your birthday?"

When the music stops, my sister sits up indignantly. "Hey."

"Yeah, I know. But I just got a call from Samantha. She wants us to come over tonight to watch movies or some crap. You up for it?"

Mattie narrows her eyes. "Since when does Samantha call you?"

I sigh. "We *did* used to be friends. Besides, she's worried about you. Come on. It'll be fun." The word *fun* feels like it's been coated in cyanide. I'm guessing Mattie's too out of it to notice how bad I am at lying, though.

"Ugh. What time?"

"She's going to pick us up at seven. That'll give you a few more hours to roll around in your own filth." I grin.

Mattie sticks out her tongue, and I take that as my dismissal.

CHAPTER TWENTY-FIVE

I stare at myself in the mirror, wondering what I've gotten myself into. A party? At Samantha's house? I haven't been there in over a year.

I get a bad case of déjà vu as I find myself wondering what shade of lip gloss I should wear. Instead, I flop down on my bed and pull out the astronomy book. The Gin Blossoms serenade me as I read about stellar evolution.

Someone pounds on my door, and then my dad sticks his head in. "Rollins is here. Should I send him up?"

Panicking, I drop my book. I don't feel ready to confront Rollins at all. I need more time to figure out what's going on, what he was doing with those pictures of Sophie and Amber. Then again, maybe this is the perfect time to grill him. I mean, if he *is* the killer, he wouldn't dare murder me in my own bedroom with my dad right down the hall. Right? Except for the fact that the killer murdered Sophie with her parents right down the hall. Shit.

Another knock.

"Come in," I yell, turning down the music.

Rollins pushes my door open, raking discarded T-shirts and music magazines across the floor. His cheeks are flaming, his hair disheveled.

"Hey," he says, a bit uncertainly. "Long time, no see."

I remember ducking down in the kitchen when he stopped by the other day. Did he catch me doing that?

"I know. Sorry. I've just been . . . busy."

The response seems inadequate. What am I supposed to say, though? *I slid into your body when you were meeting a girl who turned up dead the next day? Then I watched you give your mom a bath and found out that you have a stash of dead-girl pictures?*

"With Zane?" Rollins asks. "Yeah, I heard you two have been hanging out a lot." His brown eyes seem to darken a bit, or maybe the room just darkened a little—I can't be sure.

"Well, with Zane, but also—you know, Mattie's been going through a lot. I'm trying to be there for her." I notice he's carrying a pamphlet. Is that what he's been doing the past few days—working on a zine?

"Here," he says, holding out the booklet. "I brought this for you. Hot off the press."

I take the zine and examine it. On the cover, there's a black-and-white photograph of Sophie Jacobs and Amber Prescott in their cheerleading outfits. I recognize the picture from the pile in Rollins's room. He'd gathered pictures of Sophie and Amber for a *zine*? That's what he must have been doing with Amber on the football field that night. I remember Amber passing something to him—it must have been pictures of her and Sophie.

Across the top, in Sharpie: *Fear and Loathing in High School No. 8: The Sophie Jacobs and Amber Prescott Special Edition*. I flip through the zine. The first section contains memories about the girls from damn near everyone at East High. Next is a list of songs people dedicated to Sophie and Amber. Mattie even got in on the action, dedicating "Stand by Me" to her two dead friends. Why didn't she tell me what Rollins was doing?

Relief bubbles up inside me, and I realize just how much it would have killed me if it turned out that Rollins was the murderer. I grab him by the shoulders and pull him into a bear hug, squeezing him so hard my poor muscles ache.

"Uh, so you like it?"

"This is so beautiful, Rollins. Really." I step back and look him in the face. He seems embarrassed and pulls on his lip ring.

"I wanted to do something. How's Mattie?" He draws a Sharpie out of the pocket of his leather jacket and starts twirling it absentmindedly.

"Not that great. But tonight I'm taking her to this thing at Samantha's house—surprise birthday party. It's going to suck, but at least it'll get Mattie out of the house."

Rollins makes a face. "At *Samantha's*?"

"I know," I say, grimacing. And then I'm overcome with this intense desire to hug Rollins again, the person who knows what happened to me sophomore year, the one who's always been there. How silly I'd been to doubt him.

"I'm sorry for being a bitch to you," I say.

He shrugs. "Tough time for everyone. I get it. Hey, there's something I wanted to talk to you about." He passes the Sharpie from one hand to the other, anxiety radiating off him.

"Sure," I say, and I pull him over to my bed and sit next to him. "What's up?"

He taps the Sharpie on his thigh nervously. "The other night . . ." He pauses, starts over again. "The night that Amber died?"

"Yes?" I urge him to keep going.

"I saw her." His eyes never leave the Sharpie. "I'd asked her for some pictures of Sophie for my zine. She said she'd give them to me, but she wanted me to meet her on the football field. She was acting pretty weird."

I exhale, reassured that my hypothesis about their meeting that night was true. Unfortunately for Amber, she didn't realize she was also providing pictures for her own memorial zine.

"Weird how?" I prompt.

"Well, she told me I should tell Mattie she was sorry and that everything was her fault. And she started crying and said everyone thought she was a whore and that her whole life was a joke. I tried to tell her that wasn't true— but she got mad at me and told me to leave. I thought she was just being a drama queen, so I left her there. I never thought she'd . . ."

His hands are shaking now. "I know I should have called the cops when I heard she was dead, but I was just so scared. I thought they'd blame me or something."

I grab his hands and try to keep them still. "Rollins. Trust me. It's going to be okay. But you definitely need to tell the police what you know."

"I know. You're right. I have to tell them." It's like he's trying to convince himself.

"Hey, I'll come with you," I say. "It'll have to be tomorrow, though, because I've got to do this thing for my sister tonight."

"Vee?" He traces a finger on the palm of my hand. "I miss you."

"I miss you, too," I whisper. We sit there for a long moment, electricity flowing from his fingers to mine and then back again.

A knock on my door startles us both, and then my dad calls out, his voice strange. "Vee? You've got another visitor."

I pull my hands away and stand up. "Come in," I reply.

Zane enters the room, confusion clouding his eyes. Even though I haven't done anything wrong, I feel like I have.

"Hey," I say too loudly. "Um, Rollins, I don't think you've officially met Zane. Zane, this is my best friend, Rollins."

Rollins stands. The two eye each other suspiciously. Finally, Zane moves closer and holds out a hand, which Rollins takes grudgingly.

"Rollins was just going," I say abruptly, realizing a second too late how rude it sounds. I want to take the words back, invite Rollins to stay, but he's already moving toward the doorway. He pauses to stand before Zane.

"Be good to her," he says, an undercurrent of threat beneath his words. Before Zane can respond, Rollins disappears out the door. A sadness takes root in my belly. I'm not sure things can ever be the same between Rollins and me—not when Zane's around.

"I'm sorry," I say to Zane, even though I'm not really sure what I'm apologizing for. I just know the scene probably looked pretty fishy to him, and I don't want him to think I have romantic feelings for Rollins. He's just a friend. My best friend in the whole world.

"Don't worry about it," Zane says, wrapping his arms around my waist and nuzzling my hair. "He's protective. I get it. I would be, too."

His lips graze mine.

"Just a second," I say, pulling away and holding up one finger. I push the door closed and then melt into his arms.

Tilting my head toward my alarm clock, I see that it's nearly six. I groan, remembering that Samantha Phillips will be here to pick me up in an hour. It almost makes me laugh, to think of myself attending a cheerleader party after all this time.

Zane touches my lips. "What's so funny?"

"Ugh. I have to go to this party tonight. It's for my sister. It's her birthday."

A shadow crosses his face. "I thought you said you were worried about Mattie. We were just going to stay in and watch movies."

"I know," I say. "But it's really for the best. She needs to get out of the house. I'll be with her. Nothing will happen. You can come, too, if you want."

He pauses before speaking. "Sure. I'll come. But first could you drop by my house? There's something I want to show you."

"You could show me right now," I say teasingly, but his face remains serious. "Of course I'll come over. I'll have Samantha drop me off, okay? Then you can drive us to the party later."

Zane's face breaks into a smile. He leans over and presses his lips to mine. I sink back against my pillow, getting lost in the moment.

Just then, my door swings open. Startled, Zane and I pull apart. My dad stands in the doorway, looking partly embarrassed but mostly pissed. He clears his throat.

"Sylvia, I think it's about time for your friend to go home."

"God, Dad, how about knocking next time?" I tuck my hair behind my ear and give Zane an *I'm sorry* look.

"It's cool," Zane says, standing quickly, smoothing his clothes. "I should be going anyway." He nods at my father, muttering something about it being nice to meet him, while edging his way out of the room. "See you tonight, Vee."

My father gives me a stern look. "Five minutes. Downstairs."

I groan.

As I stand, I notice a red stain on the carpet near my bed. I kneel down to examine the spot. Unable to rub it out, I realize it's paint. Red paint.

Huh. That's weird.

Before I go down to talk to my father, I get a wet wash-cloth and scrub at the paint. The stain refuses to come out. Vanessa's going to have a shit fit.

Whenever we get in trouble, my father summons us to his office. Maybe he thinks this gives him a psychological advantage because it's his turf or something.

I hover in the doorway while he finishes typing. He makes me wait a little bit before acknowledging my presence. Then he gestures for me to sit across from him.

"I guess I haven't made a rule about boys in your bedroom," he says after a long minute. "I haven't really needed to before today."

"You were fine with Rollins coming into my room," I point out.

"Yeah, well, that's Rollins. This boy, Zane—you've never even told me about him. Then he shows up one day out of the blue and I find him on top of you?"

Heat rushes into my cheeks. "It's not like that."

"Well, what *is* it like, Sylvia?"

I look away from him. Under his desk, the crumpled photograph of the white-haired woman still sits at the bottom of his trash can. I clench my fists.

"How dare you lecture me about not telling you every little detail in my life? Between you and me, I think you're the one with the most secrets."

His glare falters, just a little, but it's enough for me to see the crack in his armor. I've found his Achilles' heel, the thing he's been keeping from us all along. Bending down,

I retrieve the picture and smooth it out on his desk.

"Would you mind telling me who *this* is?"

His face grows paler by degrees. He stares at the picture like it's something alive, something about to attack him, a wild animal.

"That's—that's all in the past," he says finally.

"*What* is all in the past?"

He squeezes his eyes closed, as if trying to block something out. "My affair." His voice is so small, I have to strain to hear it.

"Your affair? Who'd you have an affair with? This lady?"

He sighs. "Yes. But, Vee, it ended long ago."

I pick up the picture and stare at the white-haired lady in astonishment. This woman was my father's lover?

"When exactly were you with her?" I ask, dreading the answer.

"When you were little," he says softly, confirming what I'd dreaded.

"When Mom was still alive?"

He nods and reaches out, tries to take my hand, but all I see in my head is my mother at home, cancer silently eating her from inside, and him shacking up with the white-haired lady. I stand, still clutching the photograph in my hand. Scrutinizing the picture, I'm struck by the need to know the name of the woman.

"Who is she?"

"Does it matter? It's over now."

"If you've got her picture in your office, it's not over. If she's calling you, it's not over."

He looks baffled. "How did you know she called me?"

"Never mind," I say stubbornly. "What. Is. Her. Name?"

We are in a staring contest. Finally, he looks away. "Evelyn. Evelyn Morrow."

Morrow. I know that name. The name from the tombstone. The name of the little girl who died under my father's knife. He slept with Allison's mother? That doesn't make any sense. Why would he sleep with the mother of one of his patients? To ask him, though, I'd have to explain how I broke into his bottom drawer and looked through his personal papers.

Instead, I say, "Why?" I hate the way my voice sounds, like it's breaking. I hate the weakness, the hurt that coats the simple question.

His face has drained of blood. He looks like I've slapped him.

He doesn't speak.

I slam out of the room.

CHAPTER TWENTY-SIX

I stand in front of Mattie's door, staring at the sparkly My Little Pony stickers she'd decorated it with when she was little. I hear Pearl Jam's "Black" playing in the background again. I pound on the wood with the heel of my hand.

"What do you want?"

"It's almost seven. Are you dressed?"

When Mattie doesn't respond, I push into the room. She's sitting on her bed in her underwear, looking out the window into the dark.

"Is that what you're wearing to Samantha's house?"

She says nothing.

I go to her closet and look over her inventory. She hasn't done laundry in days, just tossed her dirty clothes on the floor. There are only a few shirts, a pair of jeans, and a skirt still on hangers. I pull out a pink long-sleeved T-shirt and jeans and carry them to her bed. On the way, my knees go out and my muscles turn to jelly.

The next thing I know, I'm staring into my own face as

my sister hunches over me. I've slid into my sister. I'm seeing everything from her perspective—including my own body. It's completely surreal.

"Vee? Vee? Are you okay?" She shakes my shoulders, and my eyes roll back into my head.

"Oh God. Oh God. I'm sorry. It's my fault. I'll get dressed. I'll go to the party. Just wake up." Tears splash down her cheeks and onto my face. I can't stand her feeling like this. I decide to take over, just to calm her down.

Hijacking my sister's body is about as easy as it gets. Maybe it has something to do with genes, but moving her limbs feels natural. I sit back and take a few breaths.

"It's okay," I say, even though I'm not sure she can hear me. I don't feel her there at all anymore, like she's gone to sleep or something. "It's going to be okay. Everything is going to be okay. We're going to go to this party, and we're going to have fun. Just *chill*."

When my sister's muscles have relaxed a bit, I let go of her, will myself to return. I can almost feel the energy channeling out of her and flowing back into my body, only inches away.

I open my eyes to see Mattie sitting calmly by my side. "I don't know what happened," she says, smiling. "But I feel so much better."

Samantha pulls into our driveway around 7:05. Mattie jumps into the front seat, and I skulk into the back. Samantha flashes me a totally fake smile, like the past year hasn't happened and we're still besties.

"Can you drop me off at Zane's? He's going to drive me over."

"Zane?" Samantha asks, eyeing me in the backseat.

"Yeah. He lives on Arbor." I pull the seat belt over my lap and click it in. I've seen enough of Samantha's driving to know I'm never really safe when she's behind the wheel, even if I'm only riding with her for a few blocks.

"I guess," she says reluctantly, steering the car toward Arbor Lane.

"This is it," I say, pointing.

She pulls into his driveway and barely even waits for me to climb out before she peels backward, into the street. Her car disappears around the corner, and I hear her engine revving as she picks up speed.

I knock on the door, and then stare at an ugly jack-o'-lantern carved to look like a demon. I wonder who carved it—Zane or his mother? Whoever it was has some skill with a knife.

Again, I knock, shifting my weight from one foot to the other. I need to talk to someone about what happened with my father. I need to talk to Zane.

Still, no one answers the door.

He *did* ask me to come over. Surely it wouldn't be that rude to just go in. Maybe the television is on really loud and he can't hear me. Or maybe he's upstairs.

I ring the doorbell and wait.

When no one comes to the door, I put my hand on the knob and give it a little pressure. It slides easily to the right, and the door opens just a crack. I peer in the front entryway, hoping to hear footsteps, someone coming to see who's been knocking all this time.

But no one does.

"Hello?"

Nothing.

I push the door open wider and see something strange. A tall table—the kind you might set your keys or gloves on—is tipped over, a smashed vase on the floor next to it. Shattered glass surrounds a withered rose.

"Hello?"

I step inside, eyeing the mess.

This doesn't look good. I should leave. I *know* I should leave, but something keeps me glued to the floor. I have to find Zane, make sure he's okay.

"Zane?"

I set the table upright and look around. A large open area off to the right seems to be the living room. I think I can make out the shape of a television in the dark. To my left is a staircase. The only light shines down a long hallway directly before me.

My feet carry me toward the light. I find myself in a small kitchen at the end of the hall. An olive-colored refrigerator stands in the corner, covered with little cow magnets. But most of the room is taken up by a round wooden table.

Every inch of the table is covered in papers. Bills. Junk mail. I recognize a few of Zane's papers from school. In the middle of everything is a small, generic desk calendar. Today's date is circled in red marker.

October 27.

Mattie's birthday.

Déjà vu slams into me. The white page I found on our door the day Sophie died, on her birthday. The date was circled in red. It was that piece of paper I was holding when I slid into the killer.

My knees crash onto the floor.

The paper came from this house.

The paper came from Zane.

Holy shit.

My mind reels as I search for an explanation. There must be some reason for this calendar. I mean, plenty of people must have them. Mr. Golden has one. It's just an ordinary desk calendar.

But not everyone circles dates in red.

I review the past week.

Zane's first day of school was the day Sophie died. Coincidence?

Under the bleachers, Zane rejected my theory that Sophie was murdered. Was he afraid I'd find out the truth?

The red stain on my carpet. Had he been the one to vandalize Mattie's locker? He'd had plenty of time to do it while I was in Mr. Golden's room. The blood-red paint wasn't a prank—it was a threat.

This whole time, I've been so desperate to believe a boy like Zane could ever be drawn to a girl like me. Let's face it—he's amazingly hot. He could have any girl he wanted. Yet *he* approached *me*. Was I too blind to see the real reason? All this time, was he using me to get close to Mattie?

It's *her* birthday that's circled in red. Just like Sophie's.

Oh, shit.

My boyfriend has a bizarre fetish for killing cheerleaders, and he's probably on his way to Samantha's house right this minute. I have to get there first. I have to find Mattie. The only problem is that Sam's house is on the other side of town. I'll never get there in time.

I dig my cell phone out of my pocket and call the only person in this world I can really count on. Rollins picks up on the second ring.

"Vee? What's up?"

"Rollins." I have to fight to make my words understandable because my throat has started to close up. "Rollins, you've got to help me."

"What's wrong?"

"Can you come get me? I'm at Zane's house, on Arbor. Hurry, please. I think something terrible is going to happen." I back out of the kitchen, feeling like I might puke if I look at that stupid calendar any longer.

"Are you okay? What's the address? I'm coming."

"Just hurry. Don't worry about the address. I'll be standing in front."

"I'll be right there."

Over and over, I try to call Mattie, but no one picks up. I bounce up and down, waiting for Rollins to arrive, hoping that the music at the party is just too loud for Mattie to hear her phone ring. Because I can't let myself think about the alternative.

Please. Please just let me get there in time.

"So what's this all about?" Rollins asks, steering toward Samantha's side of town.

I review the events of the last week, trying to think how to distill them into a sentence that will make sense to him. My brain is numb. It refuses to work properly. "I'm just worried about Mattie. I shouldn't have let her go to the party alone."

When we turn onto Samantha's street, we're confronted with a wall of cars. Rollins grunts in frustration, looking for enough space to park. I squirm, clutching the door handle.

"Just let me out in front. You can meet me inside."

"You sure?" Rollins asks doubtfully, but instead of a response I throw the door open wide and leap out. I steady myself and then run toward Samantha's house. Even if I'd never been here before—which I have, a million times in a past life—it would be easy to tell which house is hers. Every single light is blazing, and music pumps into the night air. There are a couple of senior boys standing on the front porch, slurping lazily from forties.

"Hey, pinky," the one wearing a football jersey slurs. "Want a beer?"

"Have you seen my sister?" I demand.

He grins. "Your sister? She as cute as you?" He reaches toward me and grabs my shoulder. I snarl at him, and he snatches his hand away. "Okay, okay. Jeez."

I push past them and let myself into Samantha's house. Music reverberates through the walls, more a feeling than a sound. I smell cigarettes and weed and stale beer and body odor.

The foyer is packed wall to wall with drunk kids. I keep my eyes peeled for Mattie, but she's nowhere to be seen. Anxiously, I push past the cheerleaders and jocks doing body shots off each other, into the kitchen, where a couple of idiots are wrestling with a beer bong.

Through the glass door that opens onto the deck, I see a snatch of white T-shirt steal behind a tree. Straining my eyes, I peer through the darkness. A figure dashes out, passing through a pool of light shining from a room upstairs, and in that split second, I recognize him.

Zane.

And he's carrying something.

I pull the door open and step into the chill of the night. The wind rustles the trees and bushes. Zane has disappeared from sight. Slowly, I cross the deck and peer over the side.

"Zane?" I call out uncertainly. "Come out where I can see you."

A figure emerges from behind a tree. It's Zane, his face illuminated by the light coming from behind me. He looks stricken. "Vee? What are you doing here? I thought you were going to my house."

"What are you doing, Zane?" My eyes fall to the red plastic container he's holding.

"You have to get out of here," he says, throwing a nervous look to the bushes behind him. "Vee. You have to run."

"I know what you did, Zane. I was there when you killed Sophie."

A look of confusion crosses Zane's face. Just then, someone else bursts out of the shadows.

It's the white-haired woman.

Evelyn.

I look from Zane to Evelyn and back again. What is my father's mistress doing here? Her face twists in rage, and she begins shouting. "What do you mean, she was going to our house? They were both supposed to be here."

My mind lingers on the words *our house*, and I'm trying to figure out what they mean when a smell, unmistakable and terrifying, rises from below.

Gasoline.

"No matter," Evelyn says. "They're both here now." She waves her arm over her head, and I realize she's holding a book of matches.

An alarm goes off inside me.

For some reason, this crazy woman is going to start a fire.

And Mattie's somewhere inside.

Who *are* these people?

And why are they doing this to us?

I spin around, knowing I have only moments before the woman throws a match on the death trap she and Zane have created. It's not enough time.

I throw open the door and start screaming. It's like I'm in a dream, yelling so loudly, but no one can hear me. They all keep smiling, nodding, dancing, talking, grinding. I push into the crowd, still yelling.

"Get out!" My voice gets sucked up in the sea of bad techno and laughter. "Get out of the house! Fire! Fire! FIRE!"

Finally, people turn toward me, their faces changing, delight melting into fear, their mouths forming Os as they realize what I'm saying. One person after another starts to echo my cry.

"Fire!"

"Get out!"

"Fire!"

One person misinterprets the situation and yells, "Cops!" but it doesn't matter. The effect is the same. Bodies scattering, pushing to get out.

Where is Mattie? Where is she?

I run down the hallway, continuing to scream. It takes all my strength to push past the people coming the other way. In the back room, slumped on a bed, is my sister. She loosely holds a plastic cup, the last dregs of a beer sloshing around inside. How did she get drunk so fast? She's only been here for an hour.

"Mattie! Mattie! Get up! There's a fire!"

Her head lolls to the side. "Vee? Whass goin on? I feel funny."

Smoke tickles my nostrils, threateningly thick.

I muster all my strength and pull her to her feet, adrenaline pumping through me. I practically carry her down the hall to the living room. Thick smoke has filled the room, but I can make out a girl lying on a plaid couch, her legs splayed. It's Samantha.

I can't just leave her here to die, but I can't carry her and my sister at the same time.

I look toward the front door, where the foyer has cleared out. I drag my sister out to the yard. Small groups of people stand around, staring at the house.

Someone is calling my name. I turn around to find Rollins rushing toward me, looking scared out of his skull.

"Christ, Vee. I thought you were still inside."

"Here. Take Mattie. I have to go back." I push Mattie into his arms and turn back to the house, which is being overtaken by flames.

Rollins grabs my arm. "What? No!"

I would be lying if I said there isn't a moment I think about just standing here on the front lawn. The night of the homecoming dance replays in my head, and I think about how Samantha just stood there as Scotch dragged me into the boys' locker room. She didn't do anything. The moment is brief, but it is undeniably there. Still, I know I would never be able to live with myself if I let Samantha burn.

"Samantha's inside," I yell, and then bolt back into the house. The air has become so toxic, I start to cough almost immediately. I cover my mouth and nose with my hand to try to filter out some of the smoke.

Samantha is still on the couch. "Samantha! Wake up!"

But she won't wake up, no matter how hard I shake her. I grab her arms and drag her off the couch. I can barely see my way to the door. Gasping, I take in a mouthful of blackness. The smoke invades my lungs, and I feel myself choking.

Everything goes black.

CHAPTER TWENTY-SEVEN

I'm standing on a dock, at the edge of a lake at the camp I went to when I was little. My dad sent my sister and me here each summer after my mother died. It was cheaper than day care. This place, on the dock, was where I'd come when I got homesick.

The only noise now is the lapping of little waves. A peacefulness washes over me. I lower myself until my belly is pressed against the hard wood and I'm able to hang my arm down and tickle the surface of the water with my finger. The lake is so cool, while the rest of my body is hot. So, so hot.

A terrible cough seizes my body, and I crumple into it. My lungs are on fire. My elbows, my toes, are on fire. When the cough ceases, I spread out my body, looking at the cloudy sky. I pray for rain to soothe my burning flesh.

Fat drops start falling all around me, bouncing off my skin and streaming onto the dock. I open my mouth, welcoming the moisture with my tongue. The rain soaks my clothes and hair.

"Sylvia." A voice sweet as honey echoes over the water.

It's my mother.

I sit up and look for her. She rows toward me in a red canoe. She guides the oar steadily through the water, first on one side of the boat and then the other. I blink, and she's here, aligning the boat with the side of the dock.

I look into the bottom of the boat and see a nest of blankets and a dark-eyed baby. My mother reaches down and snatches up the child, and then she's suddenly standing beside me on the dock.

"Would you like to hold your sister?" My mother offers the bundle to me, a gentle smile on her face.

"That's not Mattie," I say, unsure of myself.

"No. Your other sister. The one you never got to know."

My other sister? What is she talking about?

I take the child into my arms, and it weighs no more than a small sack of apples.

My mother is staring at me like she's trying to memorize my face. "You could stay here with us if you want." She sweeps her arm, gesturing to the lake, the woods, the never-ending sky.

"What is this place? Heaven?"

She shrugs.

"No offense, Mom, but I didn't like this place much as a kid, and I sure as hell don't want to spend the rest of eternity here."

She smiles. "I understand."

"I have to go back."

"Yes," she agrees. "You still have so much to do."

I start to cry.

My mother comes closer, wraps one arm around me, and rubs my back. I don't move, just soak up the feeling of my mother's hand. The baby coos in my arms.

"You've done well," she says softly.

She pulls her hand away. Even though I want to beg her not to go, I don't. How can I? She's already gone. She eases the baby back into the nest of blankets in the canoe and climbs in, one foot and then the other, carefully balancing her weight so the canoe doesn't tip.

She turns to me and blows me a kiss.

And then, she's gone.

Sirens blare in the distance, growing ever closer. The grass is cold beneath me. I roll to the side and cough until my throat is raw. Someone is stroking my hair the whole time. Foolishly, I believe for a moment that it could be my mother.

I open an eye and see Samantha's body lying nearby on the lawn. A few cheerleaders are leaning over her, holding her hand and crying.

"Vee. Say something."

I roll over and look up to see Rollins, upside down, staring at me with wild eyes.

"Is Samantha dead?"

He shakes his head. "No. Just unconscious. The paramedics are on their way."

"How did we get out?"

Rollins looks down. "I—I went in after you."

I suck in a deep breath and push myself into a sitting position so my words have full impact. "Do you know how stupid that was?"

Rollins smirks. "Isn't that a little like the pot calling the kettle black?" His face becomes serious. "Vee, don't you ever do anything like that again. I thought . . . I thought . . . Jesus, Vee, don't you know how I feel about you?"

I look away. I think I do know how he feels about me. It's something we've been dancing around, ever since homecoming last year. Maybe I've been hiding from it, unwilling to explore a connection that was forged under such disturbing circumstances, but there's no denying there's something there. Still, these are feelings I can't deal with at this moment, not while I'm lying on the cold grass after my so-called boyfriend just tried to kill my sister and a houseful of people.

Speaking of which—where the hell did Zane go? And Evelyn?

What did Evelyn say before she lit the match?

Our house. Our house. Our house.

The words march through my head.

When it dawns on me, I feel like I'm going to be sick. Evelyn, my father's old lover, is Zane's mother. Allison Morrow must have been Zane's younger sister, the one who died when he was so little. She was sick. She needed my father to save her, but he wasn't able to. And so Allison died, and Evelyn went crazy.

She yelled at Zane for trying to protect me.

She was trying to kill us.

Me and Mattie.

To get back at my father.

I feel the bile rise in my throat.

Where is Mattie? I scan the lawn quickly but don't see her anywhere.

"Rollins, where's Mattie?"

He looks shaken. "I left her right here to go in after you. I'm sure she didn't go far."

Rollins helps me to stand, and we walk the perimeter of the yard. A few people remain, but it seems most of the partygoers took off when they heard the sirens. A fire truck races down the street and stops in front of Samantha's house. A couple of men wearing thick yellow coats jump down and start unloading equipment.

I grab one of the weepy cheerleaders and ask her if she's seen Mattie. She shakes her head and turns back to Samantha.

I turn to Rollins and speak quickly. "You have to take me back to Zane's house. There's no time. Just trust me. We have to go back."

Rollins looks at me, confused, but nods. "Okay. Let's go."

On the way to Zane's house, I clutch the sides of my seat. Could Evelyn and Zane have snatched Mattie in her wasted state? Mattie would probably just go with Zane if he said I'd asked him to give her a ride home.

I have no way of knowing where they took her, but I do have the power to find them. If I can locate something at their house, something significant to Zane, I can slide into him—hopefully before anything happens to Mattie. Wrapping my arms around myself, I try not to imagine what she could be going through this very second.

After what seems like an eternity, Rollins pulls into Zane's driveway and slams on the brakes. The house looks just as I left it, the front door standing open and light from the kitchen pouring onto the front lawn.

"Come on," I say, climbing out of the car and running to the house. Rollins is close behind me. Once inside, I point out the shattered vase to Rollins. "Watch out."

I climb the staircase, two steps at a time, and pause at the top. There's a short hallway, with two doors on the left and two on the right. I try the first one on the right, but it's only a bathroom.

I try the next door. Jackpot. A narrow bed with black sheets is pushed up against a wall lined with Nirvana posters. Zane's clothes are strewn about, along with some comic books. On his bedside table is his copy of *Tender Is the Night*. It has to lead me to him. It has to.

"Okay," I say, turning to Rollins. "This is it. You just have to trust me on this. I'm going to make myself pass out. You just stay here with me, okay? If anyone comes home, shake me until I wake up. Will you do that?"

Rollins stares. "What choice are you giving me?"

"None," I reply. I grab the novel, the pages soft and worn from constant handling, and I lie back on Zane's bed. "Remember, if anyone comes, wake me up." With that, I clutch the book and squeeze my eyes closed. For a long, terrifying moment, I'm afraid it's not going to work.

I realize I'm too amped-up to slide. My pulse is racing, and I can't stop picturing what might be happening to Mattie this very second. Forcing myself to breathe deeply and slowly, I try to relax all my muscles. Rollins runs his hand through my hair, and that makes all the difference. I feel myself get drowsy.

And then the dizziness sets in, and the pain.

Black road stretches out before me. Broken bits of a yellow line disappear under the dashboard, racing under the car. Zane is on the passenger side, clutching the plastic container. The reek of gasoline makes me feel sick.

Evelyn is driving. Mattie is nowhere to be seen, I realize with relief.

Zane opens his mouth to speak. His voice is all wobbly and broken. I realize he's crying. "You didn't have to hurt her," he says. "Mattie would have been enough to get back at him."

"Dammit, Zane," the woman spits out, throwing a glare at him. "Don't you care about your little sister at all? First you try to warn them by pulling that ridiculous prank at the high school, and then you try to save that miserable Sylvia. I don't believe you. These are the people who destroyed Allison. If those girls didn't exist, your sister would still be alive. But no. Jared had to protect his precious little family, even if it meant killing his own daughter to hide his indiscretion."

"But that girl, Sophie, had nothing to do with what happened to Allison." Zane is shaking. His grip on the jug of gasoline loosens, and I realize how stupid it is to be carrying such a thing inside a moving vehicle.

Evelyn sharpens her words, flings them at him like

knives. "Nothing to do with her? You've got to be kidding me. She was born the very same day Allison died. I remember that day so well. I was sitting in the waiting room when the nurse came out to tell me my baby was dead. And Sophie's family was whooping it up with balloons and champagne. Can you tell me that's fair?"

Zane shifts the jug of gas from one knee to the other. "But the other girl, Amber. She did nothing to you."

His mother sneers. "I didn't kill her. She must have killed herself. There's something contagious about suicide, isn't there? One person goes, and it's like a domino effect."

Zane stares at his mother. "You're crazy. I should have gone to the police when I had the chance."

She slaps him in the back of the head. "How dare you call your own mother insane? Do you think I wouldn't do the same thing if someone hurt you? That's what being a mother is about. Protecting your children."

"You haven't protected me," Zane says. "You ruined me. You made my whole life about revenge. You filled my head with lies about a killer surgeon and his spoiled daughters. But you were wrong, Mother. You were *wrong*."

Evelyn stares at her son as if he's speaking another language. Zane turns his head toward the dashboard, and I feel his eyes widen in panic. Evelyn doesn't see the way the road twists suddenly to the left. Zane grabs for the wheel, but it's too late. The car shoots off the road, straight toward a tree.

The last thing I hear is Zane's scream.

And I realize it's coming from me.

CHAPTER TWENTY-EIGHT

Someone is shaking me.

"Vee? Vee!"

Rollins.

"I'm here. I'm okay," I reassure him, blinking in the sudden light of Zane's room. My head is on Rollins's lap, and his hands are cupping my face. He looks scared. I push away from him unsteadily.

Zane's scream is still ringing in my ears. I feel like I'm going to vomit.

I try to stand, but all the strength has left my legs. Rollins helps me to my feet. My hands are all rubbery, but I shove them into my pocket, searching for my cell phone. Fumbling, I pull it out, scroll down to my sister's number, and hit the Call button. The phone rings once, twice, three times . . . but no one picks up. I quickly dial our home phone number.

My dad picks up on the second ring, his voice breathless.

"Dad. Is Mattie there?"

"Where are you, Vee? I've been worried. I was afraid you were stuck in that house—"

"I'm fine. Mattie's there?" I interrupt.

"Yes. One of her friends drove her home. She's three sheets to the wind, but she's alive. Thank God. Are you on your way home?"

"Yes," I say, holding on to Rollins's sleeves for support. "I'm coming home right now."

I hang up and put the phone away.

"She's okay?" Rollins asks.

"Yes," I say. "Can you give me a ride? I just want to go home."

"Of course," he says, sounding bewildered.

I take a step toward the doorway and stumble, but Rollins stabilizes me.

"Easy," he says. "Vee, you're going to tell me what this is all about, right?"

I grab his hand and squeeze. "Yes. I promise."

He hooks an arm under my armpit. He helps me down the stairs, guides me past the broken glass, and tucks me into his car. Inside, it's warm and safe. I'm reminded of the night of the homecoming dance last year, when he rescued me from Scotch's probing hands. Just like that night, Rollins drives me home.

I lie on my bed, watching headlights from passing cars shine on my ceiling. No matter how hard I try, I can't get the sound of the crash out of my head. Zane's and his mother's shrieks, laced together for all eternity.

I called 911 to report the crash as soon as I got home, as soon as it occurred to me. The operator said an ambulance was already on the scene. I asked if everyone was okay, but she couldn't give me any details. She suggested I call the hospital, but when I did, they said they couldn't give out information.

My alarm clock blinks away the minutes, stretching them out into forever. For the first time since my mother died, I pray. I pray for Zane's life. I pray for justice—whether that means his mother's death or consecutive lifetime prison sentences, I don't know. I'll leave that up to the powers that be.

I pray for morning.

When the doorbell rings, my father is in the kitchen flipping chocolate-chip pancakes. Mattie's still asleep. Only I am left to see who it is. I pad to the front entryway in my slippers and peek through the curtain. Officer Teahen is standing there, hands thrust in his pockets, head tilted up toward the sky. I pull open the door.

"Officer Teahen," I say. "Can I help you with something?"

"Uh, Mattie?" He squints at me, like my name might be etched into my forehead somewhere.

"No, I'm Sylvia," I say.

"Is your father around?"

I nod, staring at him with wide eyes. After taking a few deep breaths, I call for my dad. He appears, wiping his hands on a dish towel.

"Officer Teahen." My father's voice is hard. "What can I do for you?"

Melting into the background, I sit on the stairs. I read a hundred different intentions in the officer's eyes. Zane and his mother are dead. The police found my fingerprints in their house and want to question me about what happened. Or they traced the 911 call and want to know how I knew about the crash. Or Zane and his mother are alive and Zane's mother wants my father arrested for "killing her baby" so many years ago.

The officer nods at my father and says, "Mr. Bell. I have some questions for you regarding a woman named Evelyn Morrow."

My father glances in my direction, then steps onto the front porch and closes the door. He doesn't return for a long time. When he does, his eyes are bloodshot and teary. He never looks like this. Never. He comes toward me, his arms stretched out like a zombie's. I don't understand what he's doing until he reaches me and hugs me until I can't breathe. But I don't want him to stop. I don't want him to let go.

"I'm so sorry, Vee," he says, stroking my hair, and that's when I know it's over. Zane is dead. I was stupid to ever think differently. Stupid to hope. I am stupid. So stupid.

My father pulls back and looks me in the face. "Zane has been in a car accident. Honey, I'm so sorry. Zane is gone."

That's when I collapse.

I awake to my father's voice.

"Vee. Wake up. Sylvia."

I open an eye and realize I'm lying on the wooden floor.

For a moment, I think this must be what it feels like to lie in a coffin, everything cold and hard.

Wrenching my head to the right, I throw up. My father holds my hair.

"That's okay, VeeVee. Let's go upstairs and get you cleaned up. Do you think you can stand?" my father asks when I'm done puking. I don't think I can. In fact, I'm pretty sure I'll never stand again. But I plant my feet on the floor and wrap my arms around his neck and—lo and behold—I'm standing. Upstairs we go, one foot in front of the other, and then down the hall to the bathroom.

My father holds his hand under the faucet until the water is just right and then helps me to undress. He looks away the whole time. And I think about Rollins and his mother and how this is just what you do for someone you love when they can't do it for themselves.

After my bath, my father helps me into my room. I let him pile the covers on top of me. He pulls the blinds tight and leaves. My eyes are wide open.

Hours pass.

I do not sleep.

Late that night, I give up on sleep and turn on my light. My bookshelf glows like it's beckoning to me. I kneel before it, looking for the book he spoke of, the one he made me promise to read again—under a tree, at dusk. My fingertips find it before my eyes do.

The Great Gatsby.

I steal down the stairs, grab my jacket from its hook and

a flashlight from the junk drawer. Careful not to make too much noise, I ease the back door open ever so carefully until the gap is just wide enough for me to slip through.

The night is cold, but I welcome it. I need to feel something other than loss, something other than pain. There is only one tree in our backyard, a great big oak tree, but it's perfect. I settle down beneath it and crack the spine on my book. It's not dusk, but it will have to do.

Just like Zane said, the experience is totally different. I'm not reading to pass a stupid English quiz. I'm reading for my life, for what Zane's life was. I'm reading to see the book through his eyes. At first, the pages move slowly, but before I know it I'm halfway through.

Soon it is light, and I'm finished. It swallowed me whole and then released me, a different person than I was before. I lie back and watch the sun inching its way upward. Maybe I didn't ever really know Zane, but on the other hand— maybe the part he showed to me was the only part of him that was real. I lie there until the sun stings my eyes, and then I pick myself up off the lawn.

CHAPTER TWENTY-NINE

My father stands in the kitchen, layering noodles on top of Italian sausage, mozzarella, and spinach. Mattie is sitting at the dining room table in front of her laptop. It is a familiar scene, but nothing about it feels right. Now that I know my father has been lying to us all these years—not only about having an affair, but also about having another *daughter*, I've been careful around him. Polite, but not overly warm.

I've decided I can't let us go on like this, living a lie. It would have been better if this was his idea, but I'm tired of waiting. I need to get things out in the open, set everything straight. So I slide onto a stool across from him. The framed picture of my mother is heavy in my lap.

"Dad? I need to talk to you about something."

He must see the seriousness in my eyes because he puts down the bag of cheese and leans forward. "What is it, Vee?"

I hold up the picture. I remove the back, retrieve the key, and lay it gently on the counter. "What's this?"

His voice is calm, and he looks me right in the eyes. "The key to my desk. I hide it because there are important documents in there, things like your birth certificate."

"Is that all that's in there?"

My sister has stopped goofing around on the computer and is staring at us.

My dad's eyes drop, can't sustain the gaze. When he looks back up at me, his eyes are full of tears. "I know it's time to tell you. I just got used to being the hero, though, you know? The man who saves babies and comes home to his beautiful daughters. Because after I tell you this, I don't know if you'll feel the same way about me."

"What are you talking about, Dad?" Mattie leaves her place at the dining room table and moves to sit next to me on one of the stools.

I steel myself. "Go on."

"I'm guessing you already looked in the drawer. You saw the medical records." He directs his words to me.

I nod.

"What's going on? What drawer?" Mattie asks.

My father takes a deep breath. "I had an affair, Mattie. Years ago, when your mother was still alive. Vee was just a toddler. Your mother was pregnant with you."

Mattie looks stricken. "You slept with someone? When Mom was pregnant?"

He looks at his hands, covered in marinara. He's clearly miserable. I almost feel sorry for him. But we need to get this over with.

"Yes. We had a fight. She was angry that I was working such long hours. She accused me of having an affair. I thought . . . I thought maybe I should just have one, since she thought that anyway."

Mattie covers her mouth with her hand. I reach over and gently rub her back. I know how shocked I was when I found out. It must be even worse for her, on top of everything she's been through lately.

"It was just the one time. But it was enough. Those medical records that you saw, Vee. The ones for Allison Morrow? She was my daughter. Your sister. She was born prematurely with a severe malformation. I was the only one who could help her. I tried. . . ."

When he breaks up into sobs, I feel horrible. No matter what he did, he's my father, and he lost someone he loved, just like I lost Mom. Seeing him so emotional tears me up inside.

"I did everything I could do," he whispers, wiping away tears, smearing tomato sauce on his cheeks. "I tried to save her."

I don't say anything for a moment. The only sound is of my father and sister crying. It's almost finished. I just need to know one more thing.

"Zane," I say quietly.

"Yes," he says, grabbing a paper towel and wiping his face. "Zane was her son."

"Why didn't you tell me? Especially when you found out we were together?"

"I—I couldn't. I wasn't ready. Evelyn started calling me, and I froze. Didn't know what to do." I try to digest this news, that Evelyn was stalking my father.

He continues on. "You can't know the guilt I've felt for these last fourteen years, Vee. It's what I think about when

I get up in the morning, when I look in the mirror. I think about it every time I scrub in to operate on another baby, someone else's baby."

I can't even fathom it, not being able to save your own daughter. Some things are too horrific to imagine, and coming from me, that's huge.

Tracing my fingers over my mother's portrait, I try to picture my dad snuggled in bed next to me and my mother, Mattie in her belly. Does the fact that my father slept with another woman take away the fact that he loved us so much? That he would have done anything for my mother? Does it take away the years he's spent taking care of us?

I look back at him, and I see my father for what he is.

A man.

He is just a man. One night, he drank a little too much and did something stupid. He made a mistake. But he is more than that mistake. He is the man who makes us lasagna, the man who holds my mother's picture and cries when he thinks no one is looking, the man who makes broken babies whole.

He is just a man. But he is a good man.

"Can you girls ever forgive me?" he asks, not daring to look up.

I climb off the stool, walk around the counter, and put my arm around him.

"Yes," I say simply.

Mattie follows my lead and tucks herself beneath his other arm. "Yes," she says.

We stand there, together, the three of us.

A family.

Marty's Diner is dead for a Sunday morning. A couple of waitresses lean against the counter, talking about the woman and boy who died in a car crash a week ago. It's been all over the news, how the cops went to the lady's house and found evidence in the basement—guns, rope, gasoline. There was also a diary filled with her mad ravings about how Jared Bell killed her baby and how she was going to get back at our family and also pretty much every kid in Mattie's grade. It was her intention to kill everyone at Samantha's party, a chubby waitress says. The tall one shakes her head, unbelieving.

Rollins sits across from me in the booth, watching me play with sugar packets.

"Vee. I'm really sorry about Zane."

I am silent.

He tries again. "I mean, I wasn't his biggest fan, but the important thing was that he made you happy. I'm sure he was a good guy. You know, despite the fact that his mom was crazy."

I try to make a little house with the packets, but it keeps falling down. I give up.

"I do want you to be happy," he says, putting his hand over mine and the scattered sugar packets.

"I know you do," I say, finally meeting his eyes. "I've been awful the last couple of weeks. There's been so much crap going on . . . but I'm sorry for being a bitch."

He taps my hand with his forefinger. "I'll forgive you if you explain to me what happened that night in Zane's room."

I sigh. I've been dreading this moment, knowing it was just around the corner but hoping I could put it off for a few more days. Today is as good as any, though.

"Okay."

I think for a minute, search for the right words.

"I'm going to tell you something about me, and it's going to sound freaking insane."

He bobs his head encouragingly. "Go on."

"Well, you know how I'm really careful about touching stuff that's not mine?"

Rollins laughs. "You mean your OCD? Yeah, I know."

"It's not OCD, Rollins. It's not narcolepsy, either. It's something else. Something I don't understand. What happens to me when I pass out—it's not right. I told my father about it when it started, and he sent me to a psychiatrist. So I don't tell people about it anymore, even though it still happens to me."

"What happens?" he asks gently.

I take the leap. "I leave my body. I slide into other people's heads. I see what they see."

Stopping for a moment, I search his eyes for that look, the one my father gave me when I told him, the mixture of fear and disbelief. But there's a different look on Rollins's face entirely. He looks concerned.

"What do you see?"

"It depends. I'll slide into Mr. Nast and see him sneaking a smoke in his office. I'll slide into my father and witness an operation. I'll slide into Mattie and see her crying at night. It's different with every person. Mostly I see things I don't want to see."

"Like what?" he prods. There's no mocking in his tone. He honestly wants to know.

So I tell him. I tell him about Amber and the naked picture of Sophie she sent to all the football players. About Mr. Golden's affair with Amber's mom. About witnessing Sophie's death. About finding out Zane's mother was responsible for everything. I tell him about my last moments with Zane.

Rollins slips out of his side of the booth and scoots in next to me. He puts his arm around me, and I can smell soap under the muskiness of his leather jacket.

"I'm so sorry," he whispers to me.

"I'm okay," I reply. "I'm okay."

It becomes apparent that the waitresses, bored, are staring at us. I nod in their direction. "Rollins, why don't you go back to your side of the table. We're turning into their entertainment."

He gives me one last squeeze and returns to his side.

Ripping open a sugar packet, he says, "So. Did you ever slide into me?" He dumps the contents in his mouth.

Shit.

The one part I left out. I know how he'll feel if he learns I saw his home life. His mother. The things he has to do to take care of her.

The fact that I don't respond tips him off. He'd been joking before, but now he's somber. "You did. Didn't you? When did you slide into me?"

"Last week," I say, squirming. It's suddenly very hot in here.

"Last week? What did you see?"

I shrug off my jacket. I don't know how to tell him I saw his mother naked, how I saw him giving her a bath. I'm boiling with embarrassment.

"Vee. Answer me."

"I saw your house and your uncle and your mother. And I know that you have to help your mom do things, like take baths."

His face is white. "You saw me . . . bathing her?"

"It's okay, Rollins. I know what it's like to take care of someone."

"Stop," he says. "You don't know. You've never had to give your sister or your father a bath. You can't possibly know what it's like. Every day. To be responsible for her well-being every single day. I have to feed her. I have to dress her. There's no one else. Just me."

I don't know what to say. "I'm . . . sorry, Rollins."

He puts his head in his hands. "I can't believe you saw me giving her a bath. I feel like . . . I feel like you *violated* me."

I reach for his hand. "Rollins . . ."

He pulls away. "No. Just leave me alone."

He rises and heads for the door. As I watch him leave, I can't help but feel guilty. He's right. I did violate him. I didn't mean to, but I did. People have a right to their secrets. The fact that I can't help sliding is no excuse.

I remember how it felt to realize Scotch was using my body without my permission. It makes me sick to think about Rollins feeling that same way. Watching Rollins drive away, I try to think of some way to make things better between us.

But I come up with nothing.

CHAPTER THIRTY

That night, I peer through my telescope, wondering why the sky looks the same when my universe has been turned completely upside down.

"Vee," my sister says. I turn to see her hovering near my doorway.

"Yes?"

She takes a few steps into my room and lowers herself into the rocking chair. She draws her knees up to her chin and looks at me thoughtfully. "Are you going to be okay?"

I look out the window again, searching. First I see Polaris, shining bright. From there, I make out Ursa Minor, the baby bear. Close by, as always, is Ursa Major. The mother bear.

"Yeah," I say. "I'll be fine. Just give me a while."

"Do you want to talk about him?"

"Who? Zane?" I turn back toward my sister.

"Yeah, tell me about him." She cocks her head to the side, the way she used to when I read her stories before bedtime.

I climb onto my bed and think awhile.

Finally, I speak. "He wasn't afraid. He'd gone through so much pain in his life, but he didn't hide himself away. Even though he knew how fragile life was—maybe *because* he knew—he seized every moment and made it his own."

She is quiet, as though she's digesting my words.

"Did you love him?"

I have to mull this over for a minute. When Zane told me he was falling for me, I was kind of paralyzed. I was so afraid to admit that I loved him, even to myself, because that would mean it would eventually all come to an end and I'd get hurt.

And that's what happened. When I found out who he was, that he'd known what his mother was doing all along, that he was just going to let Mattie die . . .

I got hurt.

Badly.

But that doesn't take away the fact that I cared for him. If only for a little while.

"Yeah. I think I did."

Mattie sighs.

We both sit quietly for a few moments.

"What happened to Rollins?"

I fluff my pillow and lean back on it. "We got into a fight. Just dumb stuff."

"You know he's in love with you, right?"

I pause.

"Yes," I finally admit. "I know."

"You should make up with him. He's a good guy." Mattie's voice is soft, and she reminds me of how she used to be as a child. Sweet. Kind.

"Maybe we will," I say, but only to appease her. Rollins has been keeping his secrets so long. I have a feeling it's going to take a while for him to forgive me for what I know.

"Hey," I say, pushing myself up. "Do you want to learn how to use Mom's telescope?"

"Sure," she replies, grinning.

I show her how to adjust the lens. She bends over and peers into the telescope, squeezing one eye shut. I watch her for a little while, noticing how she looks kind of like Dad when she's concentrating on something. She's grown up so much in the past week. Her expression is more mature. More adult. I think maybe I should tell her about my sliding sometime. Not tonight, but soon.

When my sister leaves, I lie down on my bed and stare at the ceiling, thinking about what she said—how Rollins is in love with me. I don't know that I have much to offer him right now. But one thing is for sure.

I don't want to lose him as a friend.

I turn over on my side and reach down to my backpack and pull out a notebook and pen. I flip open to a new page. I chew on my pen for a minute, waiting for the words to come to me. When they do, it's in a flood, and I have to chase them with my pen, hurrying to get them all down before they escape.

Dear Rollins,

Since our fight, I've been thinking a lot. I thought I'd take a page from your book and write it all down. I understand why you're upset, and I don't blame you. I'd be angry, too, if someone invaded my privacy like that. Still, I wish you'd been able to share your home life with me. There's so much shit in this world— what good are friends if not to help shoulder some of the burden? I guess what I'm saying is, I want you to let me be here for you. I've gotten a taste of what life is like without you as a friend, and I don't want to go back to that. I miss you. So. Much. I hope, once you cool off a little, you'll come around again.

Vee

I rip the page out, fold it in half, and stuff it into my backpack. My breath has quickened with the exhilaration of putting myself out there. It feels good. I'm not used to being so bold, but I'm proud of myself for reaching out to Rollins. It's a little scary, I must admit—who's to say Rollins won't sneer at my heartfelt letter, crumple it up, and throw it in the trash?

But maybe he won't.

EPILOGUE

Mattie and I decide our new Friday night tradition will involve board games and pepperoni pizza. Even Dad gets in on the action, after he finishes complaining that Pizza Hut can't hold a candle to his homemade Chicago-style pizza.

"Where did you get all those twenties?" Mattie asks my father in a whiny voice. "I don't think you should be the banker anymore."

I laugh, pushing my newly blond hair away from my face. Something about the transition back to my natural color just made sense. I am tired of running away from who I am. I'm ready to embrace all of me, good and bad.

I have just purchased Park Place when the doorbell rings. I toss the dice to my sister, who misses them and has to crawl under the table to find them.

"I'll get it," I say, rising and stretching.

I am still smiling when I pull open the door.

He stands there like he belongs on my front porch.

He stands there like he used to.

His hands are behind his back.

"Choose," he says.

"I've already made my choice," I say, and I grab the sleeve of his leather jacket and pull him inside.

ACKNOWLEDGMENTS

Many thanks . . .

To Sarah Davies, whom my mother once called "practically perfect in every way." Without you, *Slide* would be a shell of the book it is now, complete with an awful title. I can't thank you enough for taking a chance on a green writer. We've come a long way, haven't we?

To Julia Churchill, you pointed out the flaws and helped us make *Slide* stronger. Thanks for going to bat for *Slide* across the pond.

To my editor, Donna Bray, who loved Vee enough to bring her to life. You've challenged me to dig deep. I think I became a real writer through the editing process.

To Brenna Franzitta, Alison Klapthor, and the rest of the team at HarperCollins. Thank you so much for all your hard work.

To Megan Miranda, who stood by me every step of the way, who read and reread my drafts until her eyes were probably bleeding. Your emails keep me going.

To my other betas, Sara Raasch, Shayda Bakhshi,

Susanne Winnacker, Amber Johnston, Rebecca Rogers, Stephanie Kuehn, and Kate Walton. You believed in me before anyone else.

To my mother and sister, for loving Vee from the very start. To my brothers, for brainstorming ideas with me. To my father, for always supporting me.

To Officer Teahen, for answering my questions. I hope you enjoy your namesake.

To my extended family, and especially my mother-in-law, who ensured my house wasn't too much of a pigsty while I was busy writing.

To my daughter, for keeping things in perspective.

And to my husband, who comes up with the best ideas, who cares for our daughter while I'm locked in the revision closet, and who is my very best friend.